3 -

Life
after
Wife

Life after Wife

Carolyn Brown

The characters and events portrayed in this book are fictitious. Any similarity to real persons, living or dead, is coincidental and not intended by the author.

Published by Montlake
P.O. Box 400818
Las Vegas, NV 89140

ISBN-13: 9781612186849
ISBN-10: 161218684X

*To each and every person at Montlake Romance
who had a hand in putting this book together...thank you all!*

CHAPTER ONE

The loud, grating noise of the big black-and-chrome motor-cycle had no place at a funeral service but there it was, roar-ing into the cemetery right in the middle of "I'll Fly Away." Whoever was riding the thing had best get on down the road with his Harley. If he was still there when Aunt Maud's spirit flew away—"Hallelujah, by and by"—he would suffer a side of Sophie McSwain's red-haired Irish temper that no one, not even the head honcho of the Hells Angels, wanted to aggravate.

Kate touched Sophie's arm and whispered, "Ignore the rude idiot."

Sophie tried, but it wasn't easy when the rider parked the machine only a few feet from the grave site, hung his helmet on the handlebars at the exact moment the singers harmonized with "I'll fly away, oh glory," and squatted down at the end of Aunt Maud's blue casket.

"Who is that?" Fancy Lynn asked Sophie.

Sophie shrugged. It could not be Elijah, could it? Her glare bored into his face, but she couldn't see a thing of the man she'd met only a few times back when she was a young girl. No, that wasn't Elijah, and besides he wouldn't disrespect

Aunt Maud by riding a Harley to her funeral. The man had made a big mistake when he had squatted down beside Aunt Maud's casket. He was going to be an embarrassed Angel when he figured out that he was at the wrong funeral.

Sophie blinked and looked down at the words to the song written on the back of the memorial cards the lady from the funeral home handed to each person in attendance. Fancy sat between her and Kate, and they all three looked on together. Aunt Maud would have liked that. The three of them sitting in the chairs and sharing her service like they did everything else.

Fancy and Kate had been Sophie's best friends since grade school, and they were there to support her during the difficult time of her aunt's passing. They kept stealing glances at the man with his head bowed in reverence, as if tucking his chin against his chest would grant him absolution for all the noise he'd just made. If he thought it would, he was in for a big surprise because he was about to pay dearly for upsetting the short service. As soon as it was over, Sophie intended to tell him exactly what she thought of his rude arrival.

"Let us pray," the preacher said.

All heads bowed and Sophie tried to listen, but one eye slid open to look at the intruder. He wore a red bandanna tied around his head, do-rag style, but a few strands of jet-black hair escaped around his ears. A six-inch ponytail hung down his back and a small gold hoop hung in one ear. His cheekbones were high, his face a study in angles that left no doubt about his Native American heritage. He wore tight jeans, a black T-shirt, and plain black boots.

He looked like he should have ridden up to the funeral service on the back of a painted horse with no saddle, clad in leather buckskins with fringe on the sides, his chest bare and war paint on his face.

"Amen," the preacher said. "This concludes the service. Maud only wanted that song and a prayer. Her spirit has flown on the wings of that hymn, and there is rejoicing in heaven this morning. Sophie has asked me to announce to all of you faithful friends that dinner will be served at the ranch house. Everyone is invited."

Mr. Rude Biker raised his head and locked gazes with Sophie. Her eyes, the color of heavy fog on a winter day, did not back down from his glare. His cold, steely blue eyes looked out of place with all his other Indian features. They bore no warmth and sent a chill down Sophie's spine.

He arose from the squatting position, took two steps forward, and stuck out his hand. "You'd be Sophie McSwain? The kinky auburn hair is still the same, and those weird gray eyes. The rest of you has grown up from a whiny, leggy teenager."

Sophie rose to her feet from the folding chair in front of Maud's casket. Kate and Fancy did the same.

"And you are Kate Ducaine, the tall, dark-haired one with brown eyes, and you are Fancy Warren, the short one with blue eyes and blonde hair," he said, getting both names right.

"And exactly who are you?" Kate asked.

"I'm Elijah Jones, half owner, soon to be full owner, of Aunt Maud's ranch," he said, a big grin splitting his face and showing even white teeth.

Sophie's gray eyes turned icy. "In your wildest dreams that won't ever happen, Mr. Jones."

"I'm tougher than you are by a long shot. I'll wear you down with pure determination," he whispered.

3

"This isn't the time or place to discuss business," Fancy said.

Elijah grinned. "Just statin' facts. I'll see you back at the ranch then for lunch? Preacher said everyone was invited. Shall I stop and buy a pizza for my contribution?"

"We have plenty. You won't need to buy a thing," Kate said.

In a few easy strides he was beside his motorcycle. He threw a long leg over the seat and rode away, leaving only a puff of dust in the August heat. Texas is always hot in August, but that year it had broken all records. Farmers were to the point that they'd do rain-stomp dances for a weeklong, soaking rain. But in spite of the heat, another chill danced down Sophie's spine that morning.

She shivered and had a vision of the almighty Elijah Jones chanting for rain in full regalia like the stomp dancers she'd seen in Oklahoma at an Indian festival. Well, he could stomp. He could rev up his motorcycle engine. He could even conjure up the rain, but he wasn't buying her part of the ranch. And that was a fact!

"That was strange," Kate said.

"My worst nightmare has come true. I had no idea that man was Elijah," Sophie said.

"You knew him before?"

Sophie wiped sweat from her brow with a tissue and nodded. "I think I did, but I didn't know he was Elijah. Aunt Maud called him Bud, and I knew he was related to Uncle Jesse, but I didn't know how."

"Well, you do now, and he doesn't seem like he's in a mood to sell his half. You might have a problem," Kate said.

"He hasn't met determination, but, honey, it is right up in his face. Before the year is over, he'll be signing away his half just to get away from me," she said.

Kate chuckled. "And there, ladies and gentlemen, is our Sophie, clad in her black armor and ready for the battle that lies ahead. Aunt Maud would be proud. She can rest easy now."

"I'm going to miss her so much." Sophie's chin wobbled.

Kate touched her arm. "We'll fight him for you. He might whip one of us, but, darlin', he ain't got a chance against all three!"

"Yes, we will," Fancy said.

"He'd best bring his dinner because it'll be a long affair," Kate said.

Kate had been sworn to secrecy on her wedding day back in April and had to bite her tongue to keep from spitting out what she knew. Aunt Maud had purposely left half the ranch to Elijah and was playing matchmaker after her death. However, after meeting Elijah, Kate believed the old girl's brain tumor had affected her judgment. Elijah Jones and Sophie McSwain were as suited as a rabid coyote and a jackrabbit. Elijah would know before the first day was over that he was the jackrabbit and had better hop on his cycle and get his sorry rear end on down the road. Sophie would have to stiffen up her backbone even more if she was going to hoodwink that ranch out from under him and that big, black motorcycle, but Kate had no doubts that she was up to the task.

The three women rode back to the ranch in the funeral-home limousine along with Sophie's mother, Ellen; her father, Donnie; and her two sisters, Layla and Sandy. Kate's husband, Hart, drove their pickup truck behind the limo. Fancy's husband, Theron, and Tina, his daughter, rode in the truck behind Hart. The rest of Maud's neighbors and church family filed in behind them, creating a long procession moving slowly north from the cemetery to the ranch. The cars drove past Angus and longhorns, mesquite trees, rolling hills, ranches, and barbed wire. All a part of Maud's world; things she had loved and cussed all in a day's time. She'd left big boots behind, and Sophie wasn't sure she could fill them, but she'd never let Elijah Jones know she had a doubt in her mind.

It scarcely seemed like a year since she'd moved to Baird, Texas, population less than eighteen hundred. With her sass and frankness, Aunt Maud had turned Sophie's life around at a time when it was spiraling downhill at a dizzying speed. Sophie's preacher husband had just been killed in a plane crash—the same week that she'd found out about his affairs. As a widow she walked away with a bundle of insurance money, and he was buried with his little secrets intact.

Kate patted Sophie's knee. "We're here for you, *chère*. You've stood beside us and supported us this last year. It's our turn. You need anything, you call and we'll come running."

"And if you let that red-haired temper get ahead of you and do something drastic, just call and say that you need us to bring the shovels. We'll be there in half an hour and no one will ever find Elijah's body," Fancy whispered.

Sophie smiled.

Kate and Fancy had been her best friends since they'd started school more than twenty years before up in Albany, Texas, though the summer they were fifteen their parents all moved away from the area. They'd kept in touch through those long, dry years when they didn't see each other at all, but it wasn't the same as seeing one other every day. Kate's parents had taken her to Louisiana. Fancy's mother had moved her to Florida. And Sophie's dad had followed the oil business. First they went to the Texas Panhandle; moved to Cushing, Oklahoma, after that; and finally to Alma, Arkansas. She met her husband, Matt, in college in Fayetteville, Arkansas.

Fate had brought the three friends back to the same area the year before Maud died. Kate's father had died, and her mother came back to Breckenridge, Texas, where her family was located, so Kate made the move with her. Fancy's grandmother had fallen and broken her hip, and Fancy returned to Albany to take care of her. Sophie's world had fallen apart, and Aunt Maud insisted she come to her ranch to put it back together.

The three towns made a triangle on the map. Albany, where they'd grown up, was the uppermost point. Breckenridge was twenty-four miles to the west. Baird was twenty-five miles to the south. They met in Albany once a week on Sunday afternoons at Fancy's place to visit and kept in touch by phone or e-mails on a daily basis.

"What are you thinking about?" Kate asked.

"How lucky I am to have you two beside me," Sophie answered honestly.

"Ah, shucks," Fancy said in a slow, southern drawl.

"Don't make light of it," Sophie said. "I mean it."

Kate patted her on the shoulder. "We know you do, and we feel the same way about you."

"What am I going to do about that overbearing, insufferable hippy? You think he actually has the money to buy out my part of the ranch? I figured he'd take my more-than-generous offer and run with it," Sophie moaned.

"Elijah? How do you know he is insufferable? Maybe when he finds out just how determined you are, he'll take your money, and you'll never hear from him again," Kate said.

"Oh, he's insufferable all right. Can you believe that he had the audacity to say those things to me before Aunt Maud was even in the grave?"

Kate bit her lip to keep from grinning. Aunt Maud had known exactly how abrasive Elijah could be and probably told him to show up at the graveside service on that big cycle just to make Sophie angry. She could believe anything concerning Elijah Jones. He was simply doing what he'd been told to do, and Maud was down on her knees, peeping through the holes in heaven's floor, giggling at the chaos she'd created by dying.

"He's going to wish he'd stayed wherever he came from before the week is out," Fancy assured her.

"Where did he come from?" Kate asked.

"From the pits of Hades. When Aunt Maud told me she'd only willed me half the ranch, she said he was a military man. Maybe he still is, and he'll take my offer pretty quick. She said that Uncle Jesse had always favored Elijah over his other relatives and wanted his half left to him upon Maud's death. She abided by his wishes. I was hoping he'd be off somewhere fighting a war in the desert or jungle and would just sign the papers to get his half of the money," Sophie said.

"Guess the wish fairy was tied up," Kate said.

Sophie cut her gray eyes over at her friend. "What?"

"You said you were hoping blah, blah, blah. The wish fairy evidently didn't hear you," Kate said.

"Don't make fun of me today," Sophie whined.

"I'm not, and don't take it out on me. I didn't ask that a member of the Hells Angels show up, but I can and will help get rid of him. You just say the word, darlin', and he'll be coyote bait," Kate said.

"Sell your half to him and get on with your life," Layla said from the seat on the other side of the limo. At twenty-eight, she was three years younger than Sophie and married with three children. She and Sophie looked nothing alike. Layla had dark hair like their father, brown eyes, and a round face.

Sophie shot her a dirty look, and Layla threw up her palms to fend it off. "Hey, I'm just stating my opinion. You don't have to tie yourself down out here in the middle of nowhere. You could live anywhere with the money you have, and, if you sell your half, then that'll make you even richer. You're still young enough to find a husband."

"That's the last thing I want," Sophie said through clenched teeth.

Sandy tilted her head up and looked down her slender nose at Sophie. She was a younger version of Layla, with short, dark hair, brown eyes, a black suit, and high heels. "I understand. Matt treated you so special. It would be hard to ever find someone to replace him."

Kate almost choked on the words trying to escape from her mouth. "Don't they know?" she whispered so low that only Sophie could hear it.

Sophie barely shook her head.

"Sophie is young. She needs a helpmate. It's a long time from thirty-one to death," Layla said.

"Yes, but Matt was such a godly man. It'll be hard to find someone like him," Sandy argued.

Sophie almost bit the tip of her tongue off.

"You two leave her alone. She'll find someone if it's meant to be. If not, then it's her life," Donnie said.

"Thanks, Dad," Sophie smiled.

He reached across the space and patted her on the knee. "Sell it to the man. He wants it. You don't know a thing about ranching or cows. That's my advice. But you do whatever you want with it. I was afraid when Matt died you'd become a recluse, but these past few months you've been happy. Maybe it's the ranch that does that for you."

The smile faded. "I realize y'all want me to be happy. Right now the ranch makes me happy. The day it doesn't, I'll take Elijah's offer to buy me out. Until then, I'm not selling him one cow or chicken."

The limo came to a stop in front of the house, and the driver opened the door for the ladies. Kate slung a long leg out. Hart had already parked the truck and was beside her, hand outstretched to lead her into the house.

"How's she holdin' up?" he asked.

"Madder 'n hell. Her family doesn't understand what this place means to her," Kate whispered.

"Who was the motorcycle dude?"

"The other half of Maud's ranch. That was Elijah Jones."

"You're kiddin' me. *The* Elijah Jones? I didn't recognize him in that do-rag and a ponytail. He's aged."

"You know him?" Kate asked.

"Used to when he was a teenager and I was just a kid."

Sophie's family surrounded her when she got out of the limo. Her father looped her arm through his right one and Ellen's through his left. Layla and Sandy followed a few steps behind.

Seeing them all together, it was easy to see where Sophie got her height. She and her mother were both tall. But that's where the resemblance ended. Ellen had brown hair, green eyes, thin lips, and a weak chin.

"Where on earth did you get that red hair?" Hart asked Sophie. "No one else in your family has it."

Her father, Donnie, smiled up at Hart, who towered above him by several inches. "Grandma McSwain gave it to her. She was full-blood Irish and just about as feisty as our Sophie."

Hart continued to stare. "You really don't even look like you belong with the family."

"She doesn't," Layla laughed. "Momma found her in a bar ditch out on the other side of Albany and took pity on her since she was so ugly."

"And then she grew up to be the beautiful swan, didn't she?" Kate said.

"I'm standing right here," Sophie said.

"What did I miss?" Fancy raised her voice as she scooted her pregnant body out of the limo. Theron waited by the door and offered her his arm. Tina reached up to take Fancy's hand in hers. Even after living with her dad and stepmother for several months, Tina still felt more comfortable if she was touching Fancy. She'd spent the first three years of her life shifted from one place to the other, only to be finally abandoned by Maria, her biological mother. Fancy was her security blanket, and it was plain that all the people bewildered the little girl.

"Thought for a minute there I was going to have to call for a forklift to get you out of that thing," Theron said.

Fancy poked him on the arm. "You are so romantic."

"Momma, when are you getting that baby out of there?" Tina asked.

"Real soon," Fancy said.

Theron changed the subject. "Who was the motorcycle feller?"

"That would be Elijah Jones. He's the other half of the ranch now. He and Sophie have to share it. She wants to buy him out. He says *he's* staying and *she's* leaving."

"Elijah Jones? I've heard of that name. Hart mentioned him, I think."

"Hart knows him?"

"I just remember him saying something about Elijah. Can't remember the details. We'll have to ask him."

When they were inside the house, Sophie patted the place on the sofa next to her, and Fancy eased down between Sophie and Kate, the three women presenting their usual united front.

Mess with one and all three were there.

That's the way Elijah found them when he opened the front door and stepped inside the cool house from the blistering heat. He removed the bandanna from his head and stuffed it into his hip pocket. His thick, black hair was wet with sweat, and the black T-shirt had sucked up the sun's rays until he felt like he'd been baked inside the thing. He barely glanced at the women before heading down the hallway to the bathroom.

He found a washcloth in the same place Aunt Maud kept them when he came to the ranch as a teenager to work in the summer months. Thank goodness some things never changed.

He looked at his reflection in the mirror. No visible scars even though he'd put in three tours in Iraq and one in Afghanistan. He'd been one of the lucky ones that brought all his limbs home intact, but when he looked into Sophie's steely gray eyes, a niggling little voice said that his luck might be running pretty damned thin.

He'd hoped that Sophie would be the same whiny kid he remembered. If she'd been that girl, she would have taken his first offer for her half of the ranch and headed for the nearest shopping mall. She hated the ranch back then and carried on like she'd been sent to prison the whole time she spent there. Maybe she was playing hardball and had a higher figure in her head. Well, he wanted the ranch, and he'd have it if it took every dime in his bank account. She could just get used to the idea.

He washed his face and hands and combed his hair back into the ponytail. Using the damp cloth, he brushed the road dust from his black T-shirt. He wasn't wearing the traditional black suit, but Aunt Maud had asked that he ride his cycle to the funeral in her last letter. Somehow dress slacks, a vest, and a black suit coat didn't work with that image.

He'd wanted to come see her one more time, but he'd been undercover in one last military mission and had only gotten home from Central America two days before. He'd signed his retirement papers and made arrangements for his belongings to be moved to Baird. Then he'd driven out of Fort Hood, Texas, and headed northwest. That was the day before. He'd stopped at a motel in Fort Worth the night before and rode the rest of the way that morning.

"Here I am. Thought I'd fought my last battle, but it looks like the biggest one yet is ahead of me. I won't let you down, Aunt Maud. I'll fight her to the last breath for what you've entrusted me with. And Miss Gray Eyes can get ready to lose the war," he whispered to the man in the mirror.

Aunt Maud had left him a dream he'd never dared think about: the solitude of his own ranch. No more bombs or wars to fight. He could worry about catching a rangy, old longhorn instead of a member of the drug cartel. Sophie could either sell him her half or stay out of his way, because he wasn't budging an inch. Elijah had come home to the only stable thing he'd ever known.

He checked out the bedroom situation while he was in the hallway. Aunt Maud's was still exactly as he remembered from the last time he came for a visit. Sophie had taken up residence in the one right across the hall. That left two others. He looked into both and chose the larger one, hoping it would accommodate his furniture. He stepped off another foot on either side of the bed and determined there was room for his king-size bed that would arrive that afternoon.

He crossed the hallway and checked the other guest room. The room was big enough for an office, but the bed, dresser, and chest of drawers would have to go. He might keep the old, wooden rocking chair. He'd spent many hours sitting in it with a book in his hands.

"What are you doing? Marking your territory? Don't get too comfortable. You'll get tired of the ranch pretty quick," Sophie said.

He tensed, his hands balling into fists. No one had managed to sneak up on him in years. After two days, his survival instincts were already beginning to get rusty. "Figuring out where my things will fit, and, honey, I won't get bored. I've done my duty for my country for more than twenty years. I'm ready for boredom."

Sophie hadn't figured on him actually moving into the house. Her eyebrows drew down, eyelids shading the anger in her gray eyes. "What things?"

"The moving van should be here this afternoon."

"You mean you are moving furniture in here?" She gasped.

"That's what I mean. You got a problem with that? We will split up the house. There're four bedrooms. I'll take two. You can have two. I get half of the kitchen and half the dining room. I'll take the den. You can have the living room. What do we do about the deck? Duct tape it down the middle?"

She crossed her arms over her chest. "I thought you'd stay in the bunkhouse until I paid you off."

Elijah chuckled. "Thinking will get you in trouble every time."

"You *are* a smart ass, aren't you?"

"That would be the pot calling the kettle black, now wouldn't it? You can stay in the bunkhouse if you don't want to live with me. I snore. I get up at five o'clock every morning, and I'm not quiet. I rattle pots and pans while I'm cooking breakfast. I go for a run after I eat, and I come back all sweaty and stinky. You don't like any of the above, you go to the bunkhouse, darlin'," he said.

"Don't call me that. If it's an endearment, you don't have the right. If it's sarcasm, save it for someone who gives a…" Sophie stopped herself. He wasn't going to make her swear another time this early in the game.

"Who ticked you off this morning?" he asked.

"An egotistical fool named Elijah Jones," she told him.

He pointed at his chest. "Not me. I don't like you well enough for that."

"Believe me, the feeling is mutual. Before this goes any further, I will give you double what your half is worth," she said.

"Not interested. But if you'll move out of my doorway, I *am* hungry. I smelled fried chicken when I came in the door, so I'm going to eat. When you get ready to sell, let me know. Until then I won't badger you with offers," he said.

Sophie stepped to one side. "I will write you a check for one million dollars anytime you've had enough, and, *darlin'*, I can afford it. You let me know when you are ready to get on your expensive toy out there and ride out of Baird. Are you an idiot? This is a ranch, not a commune for worn-out Hells Angels."

"In six months we'll see who is an idiot," he said.

She let him have the last word. She'd given him a figure to boggle his little military mind. If that wasn't enough, she'd go to the bank. It was more than simply wanting to live on the ranch now. It had become a war, and after losing the last one with her sanctimonious, two-timin', preacher husband, she wasn't conceding one inch of her precious ranch to Elijah.

She marched back into the dining room where the table had been spread buffet style, and folks were helping themselves. Elijah was already visiting with Hart and Theron.

Traitors!

Tandy, an old friend of Maud's, took her by the arm and led her to the table. "Come and eat, sweetheart."

She whispered as they waited in line, "That Elijah sure grew up to be a handsome man. You'll have to be very careful living in this house with him on a permanent basis. You realize he's not really kin, and there could be talk."

"Tandy, you don't have a thing to worry about. He's not staying long enough to be a threat. I'm buying him out. And, yes, I know we are not blood kin, but believe me when I tell you that I'm flat-out not interested," Sophie said.

Tandy put a chicken leg and potato salad on a plate before handing it to Sophie. "You can add more to that, but you're going to eat that much or listen to me fuss at you. You're too thin, girl. Long legs like you got should have some meat on them."

"Are you changing the subject?" Sophie asked.

"I'm old as Maud was, darlin'. I see things a lot different than you young'uns do. So, yes, I'm changing the subject. This ain't no time for me and you to argue. But if you think you're going to run Elijah off or pay him off, sweetheart, you've got horse feathers for brains. That man has come home just like you did last year. Now, I'm going on over here and havin' a visit with Kate's momma. I don't get to see her nearly often enough," Tandy said.

Sophie wrapped her fingers around Tandy's arm. "If he's come home, then why didn't he come around while she was sick and help take care of her? If he loved this place so much and it wasn't just dollar signs to him, where was he this whole past year?"

"Ask him, not me. Elijah would have his reasons. It's the only year he didn't come see her, and most of the time he came around two or three times a year," Tandy said.

Fancy motioned for Sophie to follow her. "We've set up out on the deck. Come on out and join us. Tina has saved you a seat."

Tandy's old eyes twinkled in a bed of wrinkles. "Go on. We'll take this up later."

Sophie added a deviled egg to her plate and followed Fancy out to the deck.

"You waddle," she told Fancy.

"Are you picking a fight? I'm pregnant. All pregnant women walk like ducks. It's the forward momentum. Besides, I'm short and—why am I telling you all this? I don't have to explain to you, even if I do love you like a sister. What did that man say to you back in the hallway? You came out of there ready to chew up railroad spikes and spit out staples," Fancy said.

Sophie grimaced when she noticed that Elijah was already seated at the table with the rest of her friends. "I'll tell you later. Why did y'all invite him to sit with us?"

"Hart did it. Shoot him, not me," Fancy said.

"Why would he do that?" Sophie hissed.

"Hart's known him for a long time, and Elijah is Superman, Batman, and God all rolled up into one being. I ain't never seen Hart so happy to see a feller in my life."

"That's just great," Sophie said.

Elijah looked up. "What's so great?"

"Nothing you would understand," Sophie said.

"Hey, Sophie, do you know who your better half is?" Hart asked.

She bristled and blushed at the same time. "What did you say?"

"Just a pun on words. You two each get half the ranch, so he's your better half and you are his," Hart chuckled.

Sophie set her plate on the table and melted into the chair. She'd expected it to be one of the most difficult days in her life. Putting Aunt Maud to rest and having the full responsibility of the ranch on her shoulders would be tough. But then toss Elijah into the mix, and it turned into her worst nightmare.

"I don't know anything about Mr. Jones other than he was Uncle Jesse's great-nephew."

His blue eyes clashed with hers across the table. "Don't call me Mr. Jones. It's Eli to my friends. You can call me Elijah until you get to know me better."

She rudely ignored him. "You were saying, Hart?"

"Eli is the best bull rider I've ever seen. He taught me a lot when I was a kid. I used to come down here with Dad. Uncle Jesse knew more about farm equipment and Angus cattle than anyone this side of the Mississippi. Anyway we'd come to visit, and Eli got me started riding bulls. If he'd decided to follow the rodeo route rather than enlisting, I wouldn't have stood a chance at winning all those championships," Hart said.

"Boy, you were a natural. What you got, you did on your own. It wasn't none of my doing," Eli grinned.

Sophie gripped the chicken leg hard to keep from shoving it up Elijah's left nostril.

Sorry, God! I didn't mean to cut all his air off. I just thought he'd look cute with a chicken leg sticking out his nose. I didn't know it would kill him dead on the spot and solve all my problems. Sophie continued to ignore him.

"I can't imagine the military letting him go without a fight. He's trained more men to get in and out of tough places than you can imagine. When I was in the Guard, his name was legend," Hart said.

Everything went silent as a tomb.

Eli's gaze met Sophie's again. "Doesn't impress you much, does it?"

"Takes more than riding a bull for eight seconds or teaching a man to crawl through the jungle to impress me," she said.

"Sand," he said.

"That don't impress me much either," she said.

"It was sand we crawled through. I'm not old enough to have been in Vietnam. I did my time in the sand. Spent the last year and a half in Central America, but I didn't crawl through the jungle. Believe me there was plenty of jungle, but I didn't have to do much crawling," he said.

"There ain't no machine guns in Baird, Texas. No land mines. And no drug cartels. So frankly, my dear, I don't give a damn—as the cliché goes—what you've crawled through," Sophie said. "Just let me write you a check and you can leave."

Elijah chuckled again. "Ain't happenin'. Don't want to listen to you saying that every day so let's get it straight right now. *It. Ain't. Happenin'.* Lucifer will sell snow cones on the backside of Hades before it does. Subject closed."

He looked over at Hart. "Good chicken. Can't nobody in the world cook chicken like a Texas woman gettin' ready for a funeral. I missed southern cookin' this past year. Got tired of rice. Give me potatoes any day of the week and lots of them. Fry 'em. Mash 'em. Bake 'em."

"You got that right," Hart said.

Kate kicked him hard under the table.

"What..." he started.

"Honey, would you please go get me some of that blackberry cobbler? And I want whipped cream on the top," she said.

"Theron, would you get me a slice of pecan pie?" Fancy asked sweetly.

Elijah chuckled. "Guess that's my cue to go with them and get my own dessert. I'll keep Hart and Theron at the dessert table as long as I can so you ladies can rake us all over the coals." Elijah left his plate and followed the other two men.

"How are you going to stand it?" Kate asked.

"Not me. How is *he* going to stand it? It's not going to be pleasant, believe me," Sophie said.

"And here I'd entertained hopes that Elijah would be your soul mate. I found Theron when I came back to Texas, and Kate rediscovered Hart," Fancy said wistfully.

"You know how I feel about that preacher over in Albany that Theron likes so well?" Sophie asked.

Fancy nodded. "You haven't made it a secret that you are definitely not interested in him."

Kate giggled. "What was it you said? If I remember the words, it was 'I'd rather sit across the table from a skunk than a preacher.'"

"I'd take him over Elijah," Sophie said flatly. "That man just grates me the wrong way. The way he looks at me…"

"What?" Fancy asked.

"It…I don't know what it does…but it scares me."

Kate burst out laughing. "That's called attraction, girl. Didn't your lousy, old, dead ex-husband ever look at you like that?"

"No, he did not," Sophie huffed. "It's going to be a long winter. That's how long I figure it'll take me to wear him down. I'm so glad you two are here to support me," Sophie said.

"He's pretty, ain't he, Momma?" Tina asked.

Sophie blushed. "Dammit! I forgot she was sitting there. We shouldn't have been talking about him in front of her."

"Who, baby? That new colt out there in the pasture?" Fancy asked.

"No, Momma. That's silly. That baby horse is cute, but I was talkin' about Eli. I like him. I like his name and his ponytail. Can he come see us?" Tina asked.

"You know what they say about kids and dogs? I bet the dogs love him, too," Sophie groaned.

"What dogs?" Tina looked around. "You got dogs? Are there puppies? Can I play with them? I'll trade you one of my kittens for a puppy. Are they big puppies? Can Eli show me where they are?"

Fancy giggled.

Kate roared.

Sophie wanted to hit something.

CHAPTER TWO

Sophie sat down on the grass in front of the tombstone bearing Jesse and Maud Jones's names. The engravers would carve in Maud's death date the next week, and then it would be finished. It seemed strange to think that simply putting the date on a chunk of gray granite could finalize a lifetime. It might be over physically, but as long as Sophie was alive, she would remember her great-aunt with love. Maud had said that she wanted her life to be all used up and lived up, and then she'd slide into heaven in worn jeans and her boots ready to see Jesse again. Sophie knew beyond the proverbial shadow of a doubt that Aunt Maud had done just that. She could just see her sliding to a screeching halt in front of the pearly gates, yelling at them to open the doors and get out the salsa and chips for the party.

The sun had passed straight up and was on the downhill slide toward the west. When it came up that morning, she'd had the whole day planned and not a thing had gone according to the list. Oh yes, the song had been sung, the prayer said, lunch had been served and eaten, and the church ladies had cleaned up the kitchen. There were enough leftovers to last a week, unless Elijah ate every day like he had at lunch.

At that rate it might last two days. Kate and Fancy had gone home to their own worlds with instructions that Sophie was to call every single day with an update, and they'd see her on Sunday for their regular once a week gab fest at Fancy's place.

Her parents and sisters lingered for another hour, but then they, too, had to leave if they were going to drop Layla off in Tulsa and make it to Alma, Arkansas, before dark. Sophie was happier to see them drive away than she had been with anyone else. She'd seen her family often before Matt's death, but afterward time had drifted past. Weeks became months, and it had been a year since she'd spent time with them. Maud had told her repeatedly that she needed to come clean with her family about her dead husband, but she hadn't wanted their pity, so it was between them, like a big old Angus bull sitting right there in the living room on the sofa, every time they got together. Everyone could feel his presence, but no one talked about him. They just walked around the big critter and hoped he'd miraculously disappear.

She should have already told them about Matt, but after a year, her sisters would think she was making up stories, and her mother would never believe the pretty-boy preacher could have had a fault. It hadn't seemed right at Matt's funeral to tell her mother and sisters what a lyin', cheatin', son of a bitch he'd been. Everyone was there to bury a preacher who'd had an untainted halo and wings, so she'd let them do just that. It hadn't been difficult to let her pure, old Irish pride have its way and keep the sordid secrets hidden in her heart.

The first time she'd told anyone other than Maud the whole story had been a year before, when she and Kate had met Fancy at her grandmother's house for a reunion. Kate mentioned an old country song entitled "80's Ladies." The singer mentioned three little girls from the fifties and said that one was pretty, one was smart, and one was a borderline fool.

As sweat ran down Sophie's neck and into her bra that summer evening at the Baird cemetery, she recalled the day that Kate had said that Fancy was the pretty one, Sophie was the smart one, and she was the borderline fool. Sophie dang sure didn't feel so smart right then.

There had been a slight breeze to rustle the leaves in the pecan tree above Maud's grave, but it died. Sophie ran her hand across her forehead and pushed back a few errant hairs. Summertime sweat was as sticky as superglue. Her kinky hair kept sneaking out of the ponytail and plastering itself to her neck. Come evening time, it might take acetone to get her bra peeled off her skin. Even her denim shorts were sticking to her thighs like flies on the remnants of a snow cone.

She leaned forward and ran a finger over Maud Jones's name.

The funeral service had been exactly what Aunt Maud had told her to arrange.

"I don't want a big church funeral with all that snot slinging. Just let everyone meet at the cemetery, sing 'I'll Fly Away,' and let the preacher pray over my dead body. The song is for closure, and the praying is to make him and everyone else feel better about me going. Remember, Sophie, I'm dead. Go on with life. Enjoy it. Savor it. When the end comes, go out with a shout and slide up to the pearly gates with no regrets. That's what I'm going to do," she'd said that last week of her life.

It was as if Sophie could hear Maud's voice behind her, repeating the words she'd said the day before she died. "Don't you put me in no brand-new suit. I never wore a suit to anything in my life. Barely could abide a dress at funerals and for church. You bury me in my jeans and shirt, and don't forget my boots. That old pair with the scuffed heels. I've got some work to do up there before my friends arrive, and besides, Jesse is waiting to dance with me. I can't dance barefoot. He loves to dance, but he steps on my toes pretty often. And I sure can't dance in new boots. I'd have blisters for sure. Promise me." Aunt Maud had held her hand tightly until she got the promise.

Sophie touched the tombstone. "What am I going to do? Why didn't you just leave the whole thing to him instead of giving me your half? I'm not strong enough to do this."

A hot wind stirred up a dust devil on top of the new grave. Sophie was mesmerized as she watched the miniature tornado in front of her. Then she recalled Aunt Maud's speech from when Matt died. Maud had flown from Dallas to Tulsa for the funeral. She'd arrived a few hours ahead of Sophie's parents and her two sisters. Sophie had poured out the story, and Maud had taken control.

"God has a special place reserved for men who are in the preachin' business for the glory and the money. Matt didn't have no calling to the ministry. He had dollar signs and power in his eyes. You are going home with me and getting over this with some good old, hard, physical work. Let him have his final minutes of glory and you play the bereaved widow for the cameras. There's a strong woman in you, Sophie McSwain. We're going to find her. That man might have stomped you down for a few years, but you can come back with some help and I'm here to help you."

After the funeral she'd gone home with Aunt Maud, and the past year she thought she'd found that strong woman, until that morning when she'd squared off with Elijah. Now she wasn't so sure about any of it. The strong woman might only be there when there were no storms, and the first sign of a strong wind would knock her flat on her butt.

"No, I will not," she said vehemently. She couldn't let Aunt Maud down, not even if she was dead and gone. She had to show her that she could still be strong.

She touched the tombstone once more and got to her feet. She squared her shoulders and headed for her truck. The storm that hit after Matt died was an emotional hurricane, and she'd survived it. She would come out on the other end of the one ahead of her with a ranch and even more strength. If it don't kill you, it'll make you stronger. She forgot who said those famous words but she'd live by them, and when it was all said and done Elijah Jones would be riding out of Callahan County with his pride hanging from his handlebars.

He'd said the moving company would be there by evening, but she was shocked to see the big truck sitting in front of the house when she got back to the ranch. Elijah and two other men were busy taking things in and bringing other things out. A bed, along with the mattress and box spring, was sitting on the porch. A dresser stood like a lonely sentinel in the yard, and they were bringing out another bed.

"What in the devil are you doing?" Her voice squeaked like a little girl's on the playground at recess.

"I'm moving in. I told you this morning the movers would be here. I decided my two bedrooms could be across the hall from each other. That way you can have the one you occupy now and Aunt Maud's. I have an ulterior motive. I don't want to deal with cleaning her things out," he said.

"Why do you need two?" she asked.

"One for the bedroom, and one for my personal office. We can share the ranch office. If you want a personal one, then you can put it in Aunt Maud's old room," he said.

"Have you no shame? She's barely in the grave."

"Her last letter said to get on with business after the funeral. Today I'm moving in. Tomorrow we're walking over as much of the ranch as we can, or we can ride four-wheelers to make it easier. The next day you are showing me the accounts. That's called getting on with business," he said.

She glared at him.

He shrugged as if her dirty looks weren't even as important as a gnat buzzing around his ears. "I'm going out on a limb here and being nice. It's not easy and it's not part of my personality, so don't expect it again. What do you want done with what I'm taking out of here?"

"That's not nice. That's business," she protested.

"Yes, it is nice. Is anything out here your personal property, or is it ours jointly because it belongs to the estate? Tell me or the movers will put it in the truck and take it to the nearest shelter for the homeless." He crossed his arms over his chest and waited.

"They're not my personal things, but I don't want them given away. Store them in the bunkhouse for now," she said.

"You heard the lady. Put them on the truck and take them around back and down the lane. You'll see a long, skinny house back there. I left the door open when I checked it out a few minutes ago. Just stack them up anyway you can, and she can have the hired help do whatever she wants with them," he said.

She continued to glare at him. Why did someone that handsome have to be such a pain? If he chopped off the little sissy ponytail and had his hair cut in a feathered-back style, he'd be close to movie-star good-looking. The cameras would love those high cheekbones and that chiseled face. He could use a little more in the lip area, but the slight cleft in his chin and those blue eyes made up for the thin, firm, no-nonsense mouth.

"Might as well stop giving me your meanest looks. I've been hated by professionals, lady, and you are just an amateur. I don't care if you like me. I don't care if you hate me. We'll have to work together until this is settled. All the rest is small stuff, and I don't sweat the small stuff," he said.

From behind his dark sunglasses, he scanned Sophie in her tight jean shorts and bright green, stretchy tank top without her knowing it. She'd grown up to be a beauty, no doubt about that. She'd been a skinny kid that reminded him of a newborn colt trying to grow into a set of long legs. Well, she'd done the job very well. Her unruly curly hair begged a man to tangle his hands into it, her lips were made for kissing, her legs reached halfway to heaven, and her gray eyes saw straight into his soul. How on earth that man she was married to could cheat on something that gorgeous had to be a total mystery. He had to be an idiot, but Aunt Maud said he was a well-respected preacher. It only went to prove again that you can't judge a book by its cover or a man by his lies.

She sighed when he didn't say anything else. "It's a necessary evil, but I don't have to like it."

"No one said either of us had to like it. You want to empty those drawers before they load that dresser?" He tossed her a box he no longer needed.

"No, I don't but I will," she mumbled.

What she found barely filled half the box. All the drawers were empty except one, and it held a few dresser scarves and hand-crocheted doilies. Maud might have used them when she and Jesse first took up housekeeping, but in the years Sophie had known her there hadn't been any "foo-rah," as Maud called it, in the house. Her tables held basic items: lamps, ashtrayst from when Jesse was alive, candy dishes that were always full, coasters, and magazines.

"It's ready to go," Sophie said when she finished.

"The guys in the bunkhouse going to mind all this extra stuff?" Elijah asked.

"There are no guys in the bunkhouse. We hired on extra help for the summer, but they come and go every day. No one lives in the bunkhouse anymore."

Elijah raised an eyebrow. "Foreman?"

She shook her head. "Aunt Maud and I managed it on our own. Better equipment these days than when Uncle Jesse was alive. The ranch has moved into technology. We keep things on the computers, back them up on flash drives at the end of each week, and only hire outside help for seasonal work. We'll need extra in three weeks for the cattle sale. Why? You want to change your mind? You don't get to boss around a whole bunkhouse full of men. We had six that came every day during the summer months. Three of those are back in high school. Two went back to college."

"Gus?"

"He's the full time, but he got married last year."

Elijah stammered. "But he's got to be sixty years old. No, he's older than that, isn't he?"

"So does that mean he can't fall in love?"

"My hero has bitten the dust," Elijah said.

"Is that a whine I hear coming from the big, old he-man?" Sophie asked.

"It could be, but it'll only last a minute. Who'd he marry?"

"Lady over in Clyde. She's a retired schoolteacher. Never married. No kids, of course. Thinks Gus hung the moon."

Elijah mopped sweat from his forehead and shoved the red bandanna back into his hip pocket. "He did at one time. I'm not so sure anymore since he let a woman brand him. But at least he still comes to work every morning, right?"

"He was at the funeral with his wife. Didn't you see him? Her name is Alma Grace."

"Guess I didn't. But I will tomorrow. We'll wait until then to talk business. Do you want these men to take Aunt Maud's things out of her room and store them in the bunkhouse?"

"I. Do. Not! I want to keep her spirit in there a while longer," Sophie smarted off at him.

"It's *your* other room. Do with it whatever you want, but don't be begging me to help carry things to the bunkhouse when you get a wild hair and want that room for a sewing room," he quipped right back at her.

She took two steps toward him and tiptoed until her face was just inches from his. "I don't sew. I'll do my share of the housework, but you will help. I'll help work cattle, put up hay, drive a tractor. Anything you can do, big boy, I can do better, so don't be thinking I'm a little stay-in-the-house woman. If you've got a problem with helping to cook or washing dishes, don't let those men leave until they've reloaded *your* things."

He leaned down until his nose came so close that it became two when she tried to focus on it.

"I bet I'm a sight better housekeeper than you are, and I hate things out of order, so put that in your big-girl pipe and smoke it, sister. And I can sew when I want to, so add that to my list of accomplishments."

"Honeymoon must be over," one of the movers laughed.

"Honeymoon ain't even started," Elijah growled.

"Honeymoon ain't never startin'," Sophie hissed.

The movers all chuckled as they went back to the truck for another piece of expensive furniture, this time a leather recliner that had seen lots and lots of wear.

"Where do you want this?" two of them asked at the same time.

"In the den and take out all the furniture in there," Elijah answered.

Sophie turned around abruptly and stomped into the house, slamming the screen door behind her. She watched the men as they placed the recliner where the old, brown, plaid one had sat as long as she could remember. In that moment she realized how badly she hated change. That's what had kept her head buried in the sand all those years with Matt. To acknowledge that the only time her marriage was happy was when he was in front of the cameras on Sunday morning would mean she'd have to change things.

"That's good. Right in front of the big-screen television," Elijah said right behind her.

She pointed. "You see that little burgundy recliner over there by the bookcase? You move it one inch, and I'll spend the rest of my life in jail for killing you. That's not a threat. It's a promise that you can take to the bank. I mean it. That one is mine."

He narrowed those cool blue eyes until they were little more than slits. "The living room is yours. The den is mine. Take it to the living room."

"That was *your* idea, not mine. I love this den. It's where I spend my evenings, and I'm not budging. Get out the duct tape, and we'll mark off half the room. You can have half the formal living room, but you are not moving the sofa either," she said.

He bit his lower lip. "You are a spitfire."

"You are the devil."

"OK, the ugly purple recliner can stay. Anything else you're going to have a fit over?"

"The bookcase can't be touched. I don't care if you bring in your ugly, old, modern big-screen television, but you touch that rug in front of the fireplace, and I'll poison your iced tea."

"I don't drink iced tea. I like ice-cold Dr Pepper," he said.

"You can go to…" she stopped midsentence.

He chuckled. "I thought you were a preacher's wife."

"I thought you were a…" She couldn't think of a word ugly enough to say. Not even her extensive repertoire of cuss words had one that would describe Elijah.

"I'll let you think about that while I go tell these guys where I want the rest of my things placed," he said.

Suddenly, Sophie was starving. She hadn't known true hunger since the policeman knocked on her door and told her that there had been a plane crash. Fancy ate like a horse when she was upset. Kate always ate enough for two field hands. But Sophie ate when she had to, not because she wanted food.

She marched into the kitchen and opened the refrigerator. She piled little containers of leftovers on the cabinet and got a fork from the drawer. Cold chicken wasn't bad at all; neither were baked beans or potato salad. When she took the top off some sauerkraut and hot links she paused.

"No guts, no glory," she mumbled as she dug in.

"Wow! Even that's good. Standing up for myself gave me an appetite! By Christmas, I may be calling on Omar the Tentmaker to make my clothes if it's always like this," she said when she'd chewed the first bite.

Elijah helped carry in his television and his sofa that matched the recliner. True to his word, he didn't touch the ugly chair over by the bookcase. He scanned the titles, surprised to find several of his own favorite authors scattered among the familiar old classics that Maud had read and reread.

He'd finally accomplished his goal and made Sophie mad enough that she'd stormed off in a snit. Now he could do what he wanted with the den. The sofa needed to be exactly the right distance from the television to get the full effect of the big picture. The stereo system went into the corner where an antique secretary had sat for so long that there was a light spot on the carpet when they took it out of the room. He put on a Zac Brown CD and turned the volume to the right loudness as the guitar music started. He wiggled his head to the lyrics as Zac sang "Colder Weather."

Elijah loved the mountains in Wyoming and Montana, but he wouldn't want to live there forever. Still, the song reminded him of the times he'd taken his vacation time and gone to a cabin in the mountains and watched the sunset over the snowcaps. He sang loudly with Zac as he arranged things just so.

Sophie heard the music and carried the bowl of cold sauerkraut to the den. She could hardly believe that Elijah would like that particular band. Hard rock went with his motorcycle image, not Zac Brown.

When he felt her presence, he turned quickly and almost blushed.

"I like this group," he said.

"You couldn't carry a tune in a bucket with the lid welded shut," she said around a mouthful of kraut.

"Who cares? I love to sing, and that's all that matters," he said.

"You are off-key and out of tune," she said flatly.

"So what?"

"Turn it down."

"No. I like it loud. You don't like it; you can go outside and pout."

She looked around at the den. It did look better. The leather brought out the dark, raised panel walls. The television didn't even look out of place set in the rustic entertainment cabinet system with doors that could close off the screen.

Zac began to sing something about getting away to where the boat leaves from. She'd like to get away to anywhere, but not forever. Ranching was in her blood, and in the past year she'd been more alive than ever. If she sold out, she'd never know what the rest of her life was supposed to be like.

"Well? You going outside, or are you going to bring me a Dr Pepper and listen to the CD with me while I take a rest? The movers are taking the other furniture to the bunkhouse," he said.

"Get your own soda pop. I'm not your maid or your wife. There ain't enough money in the world to pay me to be either."

He popped the footrest down and headed for the kitchen. "Honey, there ain't enough money for me to pay you to be either one. Anyone who'd eat cold kraut is crazy as an out-house rat."

She followed him. "You are lucky you've even got Dr Pepper. Aunt Maud and I like Pepsi. Someone just happened to bring in a six-pack of Dr Pepper for the funeral."

Elijah deliberately eyed her from toes to eyeballs, this time without his sunglasses. "I would have pictured you with an ale in your hands instead of soda pop."

"I'm half Irish, and believe me, if push came to shove, I could outdrink you any day of the week. Indians don't hold their liquor worth a dang." She shoved the fork into the kraut and brought up another mouthful.

He snarled. "That is disgusting."

"You are changing the subject because you know I'm right about the drinking."

"I do not drink, Sophie. In my profession, we had to have a steady mind and hand. Drinking didn't go with it, but it had nothing to do with my Indian blood. I'm going to have a Dr Pepper," he said.

"What're the other genes?" she asked.

"Momma was a Whitehawk before she married Dad."

"Chickasaw?"

"No, she was full-blooded Fox Indian from up in central Oklahoma. You got any smarty-pants remarks, say 'em now and get 'em out of your system. I don't take teasin' about my heritage."

"Neither do I. First time you call me a Paddy, I'll slit your throat in the night with a rusty knife. So you got anything to say about my Irish hair, my freckles, or my eyes, lay it out on the table now."

Elijah almost grinned. Aunt Maud had been right when she said she was bringing the girl up out of the pits. She was hot-tempered, hot-looking, and there was no way she would ever let herself sink into the depths of despair again. Not Sophie! She was a full-fledged bag of pure sass.

"You don't mention my ponytail, and I'll keep quiet about your Irish-Afro hairdo," he said.

"You got a deal. You want something to eat, get after it. There's the microwave." She carried her food out the back door to the deck, where she sat down in a lounge chair and propped her feet up. She'd never felt so alive in her life. Maybe she should eat kraut every day.

CHAPTER THREE

Sophie was sitting at the kitchen table, laptop in front of her, along with a cup of steaming black coffee and an empty plate. The aroma of bacon and hot biscuits filled Elijah's nose when he stumbled into the room at five o'clock.

He was dressed in plaid cotton lounge pants and a white gauze muscle shirt that stretched across every well-defined muscle in his chest. Two major scars were visible. A long, skinny, white one on his upper left arm and a pockmark on his right shoulder.

Sophie didn't see a single tattoo, which surprised her. Didn't all military personnel prove how mean and tough they were by having some kind of art stamped on their body? Maybe he'd had his done where she couldn't see.

If he noticed the blush, she hoped that he chalked it up to the heat in the kitchen.

"Good mornin', sleepyhead. You always sleep until the sun rises?" she asked cheerfully.

He yawned. "The sun won't be up for a couple of hours. What are you doing? Trying to get a step ahead of me?"

"Wouldn't have to work too hard at that. I get up at four thirty every morning. Breakfast is always at five because that's what Aunt Maud liked. There're biscuits and bacon on the stove. Sausage gravy in the pan on the back burner. You want eggs, you cook 'em."

He poured a cup of coffee, sat down at the table, and pointed. "What's that for?"

"It's the ranch laptop. You can glance over it while you wake up. It's got the financials, the bank balance, the savings accounts, CDs, and such in it. There's another one for each cow or bull on the property. Hard copy is in the file cabinet in the office. Along with her stock portfolio. She didn't take risks with those, so we're in good shape. Password: Jesse. And I keep the files backed up, like I said, on a flash drive. I'm going out for my morning run now. You take your time. I'll gas up the four-wheelers for the survey you wanted."

"Why are you being nice?" he grumbled.

"I'm not. I want you to know exactly what this ranch is worth and what a good deal you'd be getting if you took me up on my offer today. It's going down ten thousand dollars a day until there's nothing left," she said.

"It ain't happenin'."

She ignored the remark. He wasn't going to rile her. Anger would only lose her points.

He slid a glance at her as she left. Boxer shorts with a picture of Minnie Mouse on the butt were a size too big, and long legs shot out from below the wide legs. Her bright orange knit shirt with no sleeves hugged her slim body, nipping in from well-rounded hips. Her kinky red hair looked like someone had combed it that morning with a hay rake.

He'd seen confidence leave a room before, but never in that measure. She had no doubt that she'd wear him down with her constant badgering to sell out, but like he kept telling her, it wasn't happening. She would have to learn that he wanted the ranch ten times more than she did. He didn't care if she subtracted a hundred thousand dollars each day. He had come home, and peace did not have a price tag hanging on it.

He fried four eggs over easy. While he waited on them to cook, he loaded up a plate with sausage gravy over biscuits and strips of crispy bacon. When the eggs were ready, he added them to the plate, poured another cup of coffee, and carried it all to the table. He'd have to run an extra mile after eating so much, but it smelled so good.

By the time he finished eating, washed his dishes, and scanned the financial report—which sent his eyebrows to the ceiling more than once—Sophie was back from her morning run. He didn't see her but heard her whistling in the shower when he passed the bathroom. He hurriedly changed into his running shoes and clothing.

Sophie finished her morning shower and dressed in jeans and a T-shirt, pulled her hair up into a wet ponytail, shoved a few pins in it to hold a bun in place, and shoved an old straw hat on her head. She burned easily and never tanned.

Burn. Peel. Burn again. That was what Sophie did! She'd cut off her pinky toes for Kate's skin. Kate's mother was Mexican, so Kate had that coffee-with-heavy-cream skin that looked like she'd been in the tanning bed all the time.

She heard Elijah slam the front door as she went out the back one. Sophie loved Texas sunrises and sunsets, and that morning there was a fantastic show in the east with all the gorgeous oranges and pinks.

Was Elijah even appreciating all the beauty in front of him? What kind of name was Elijah anyway? Of course, it came from the Bible. She'd been dragged to church often enough to know that much. But who, in these days, named their child such an antiquated name?

"OK, so it's not *these* days, and his momma hung that on him forty years ago," she mumbled on her way to the shed where they kept the three four-wheelers. Still, the idea of looking down into the face of a newborn, squalling baby boy and giving him a name like Elijah kept running through her mind.

Maybe he hadn't ever been a baby. Maybe he'd been tossed onto earth from an alien ship in an egg, and when some redneck farmers out in the backwoods cracked it open, out popped a full-grown man in military garb. They named him Elijah because they thought he'd been heaved to earth from heaven. They didn't know what to do with him, so they took him to the nearest military establishment and handed him over to them.

It made more sense than a little boy starting kindergarten and telling his newfound friends (named things like Kyle and Mark and Jimmy) that his name was Elijah. That could be what made him so edgy—having to take up for himself when the other kids picked on him about his name. Well, she hadn't had it so easy either with a name like Sophia. It sounded like an old-maid schoolteacher with a gray bun and a hook nose with reading glasses perched on the end of it.

"What are you thinking about so seriously?" he asked, so close to her neck that the warmth of his breath brushed across the tender skin.

"My name," she said. She'd thought that he was out for a run.

He should be shot between his pretty blue eyes for sneaking up on her like that and asking a question that she didn't have time to think about. Thank goodness he didn't ask her anything important. She would have blurted the answer out like an honest, little three-year-old that hadn't learned to lie.

"Sophia Lauren McSwain. What's wrong with that?" he said. "Where are we starting this tour of the ranch?"

She took two steps forward in pretense of checking the tires on the four-wheeled vehicles. "Not one thing is wrong with my name, but it's not something that you tag on a little girl in today's world. I'm not ashamed of it, but I wouldn't name a kid something that would get them teased at school," she said.

"Why were you thinking about your name?"

"Full of questions aren't you? You thinkin' you will file away any information I give you and use it to coerce me into letting go of my half at a later date?" she asked.

"Later date? I was hoping to do so today," he answered.

She giggled.

The sound of her laughter sent his anger level up a notch, but true to his heritage he kept a stone face. "Is this going to take all day, or will we be back for lunch?"

"We'll be back. First of all, I'm mean when I'm hungry, and even Aunt Maud didn't keep me out on a job without making sure I got food. Two, it's going to get almighty hot by noon."

"You got the work narrowed down to where you don't have to do anything when it's hot or cold? Can't take the weather?" He mounted a vehicle and turned the key to start the engine.

She did the same. "I can do anything that keeps this ranch going. Don't get your hopes up, chief."

"I thought we'd settled that business of racial slurs," he growled.

"OK, then don't get your hopes up, period. Want me to lead?"

"I know the layout of this place as well as you do. Maybe better. You can follow," he said.

"Not me. I don't follow anyone anymore," she yelled over the roar of the engines.

They rode side by side down the west side of the ranch, checking the fence as they went. Only once did she stop and fix a broken barbed wire with the equipment she kept in the saddlebags behind her seat. He watched, prepared to step in and finish the job when she broke a nail or scratched her hand, but she did the job expertly, with no problems.

"You can take care of the next one," she said when she was ready to ride again.

"You think I can't fix a fence?" he asked.

"I think you can do anything on this ranch. If you'd been lazy, Aunt Maud wouldn't have let you come back after the first summer. Seems I remember you bein' here every time Momma made me come spend a week or two. Only then Aunt Maud called you Bud, not Eli or Elijah," she said before she started the engine.

He threw one leg over the seat like he would if he'd been sitting in a saddle on the back of a horse. "Uncle Jesse called me his little buddy when I was little. I grew into Bud when I was a teenager. So there's a bit of information for you."

"I remember you being a hard worker. That's a good thing. I can always use a good hand on the place," she said.

A sly grin tickled the corners of his thin mouth. "I remember you being sassy and bored to tears, which isn't a good thing. But you can fix a fence and keep pretty good records, and I can always use a person like that on the ranch."

"So are you making fun of me or hiring me? I didn't even know there was a position open," she said coolly.

"Right back atcha, darlin'. You tryin' to hire me? I don't work cheap," he said.

"Touché, darlin'! We each got a point and lost it. Let's go check on the rest of the place," she said.

It was eleven thirty when they completed the tour. Elijah was pleased with what he saw. The war against the prolific mesquite trees hadn't been won, but Sophie and Maud had kept it in check. The cattle were fat and well fed on pastures that were still producing. The calf crop for the fall looked good and profitable. He'd already begun a mental list of the bulls and the cows that should go to the sale.

She parked her vehicle beside the yard fence. He did the same.

"We'll clean them up and refuel after we eat," she said.

He nodded in agreement.

Things were the same as the last time he'd been to Baird, Texas. That was a good sign in his books. Steady and sure. Peaceful and home.

She washed up at the kitchen sink and dried her hands on a tea towel, wasting very few motions. He watched as she removed containers from the refrigerator and opened them.

She motioned toward the cabinet top. "You are a big boy and know how to use a microwave. Fix yourself a plate from the leftovers. We don't waste much around here."

"It's good food. Be a shame to waste it." He remembered many times when he would have given half his bank account for leftovers from Aunt Maud's refrigerator.

Their hands brushed when they both went for a slab of ham at the same time. Sparks flew, but she attributed it to anger. He figured it was the result of looking at her long legs too much that morning.

She pulled a can of Pepsi from the refrigerator while her food heated in the microwave and set it on the kitchen table at one end. No way was she conceding the head of the table to him on the first day.

He fixed a plate and set it beside the microwave to wait his turn and got a can of soda pop from the fridge. He set it on the other end. He wasn't about to take a lesser place and sit on the side.

"So tell me, who are you dating? That preacher man from over in Albany?" Elijah asked.

Her jaw began to work in a fit of anger. "What makes you think I'd date another preacher? Or that I'm dating anyone? This ranch takes all my energy and time. Keeping it running smoothly and taking care of Aunt Maud didn't leave time for men."

"I understand it left Sunday afternoons. You have time for those two girlfriends of yours; you'd have time to date. Unless you like the girls better than you do men folk?"

"You are not going to fire up my anger, Mr. Jones. I like men just fine. I might even like one well enough to date someday. But not now," she said.

"Why? You aren't that ugly that no one would want you. You landed that television preacher easy enough," he said.

That ugly! So that was his opinion of her.

The microwave buzzed. She removed her plate with hot pads and carried it to the table. "Matt taught me a hard lesson. Don't trust."

He set his food inside and turned the dial to three minutes. "So what's it going to take for you to trust?"

"Kate, Fancy, and I had this conversation a year ago. Kate said a man had to ride up on a white horse and be her knight in shining—and then she couldn't think of the right word, so she said 'whatever'—and make her truly believe in the words 'I love you.' Well, it took Hart a while to convince her that he was her knight in shining whatever, but he did finally. And Fancy said that someone had to offer her a forever thing."

"What in the devil is a forever thing?" he asked.

"It's a thing that lasts way past attraction and saying the vows in front of a preacher. It's something that endures the fights as well as the good times right up until the last breath is drawn. That's a forever thing," she answered.

The buzzer went off again, and he took his food to the table. "I didn't ask about your two best buds. I asked about you," he said.

"I thought Native Americans had the patience of Job. That they could sit beside a tree for six weeks waiting on a deer to come by." She picked up her fork and began to eat.

"You trying to psych me out by making me wait. You might be surprised," he said after a few minutes.

"No, just deciding whether I want to share even this much about me with you. Evidently you already know more about me than I do you."

"Aunt Maud wrote to me every week. I did the same unless it wasn't possible for security reasons. Last letter I got was a week before she died. She told me exactly what to do and what she planned."

Sophie filed that bit of news away with the intention of turning Maud's room upside down for those letters. Maud never threw a thing away, so they'd be stuffed somewhere, and Sophie fully intended to find them and read them!

"OK, we called them our three magic words. Mine was *life after wife*. That's what it'll take for me to ever trust a man again. So I don't have to worry about ever marryin' another fellow. Because there's not one out there who can give me that," she said between bites of ham, candied yams, and cranberry salad.

"What do you mean by those words? Life after wife? Doesn't make a bit of sense to me," he said.

She sighed. "'Life' as in living and breathing and compan- ionship and trust. 'After' as in after the wedding ceremony. 'Wife' as in opposite of husband."

He looked up with questions written on his face.

"A man would have to prove to me, beyond a doubt, that he was giving me a life after the wedding. My dead husband showed me that the title of wife doesn't necessarily mean much. I want the courtship and the dating and all that romance. But then I want a promise that it will go on after I get the wife title. I want the romance to extend past the day when I stand up before the preacher and vow to love some old boy forever, amen."

"I think I understand," he said.

"I doubt it. Men do not have the ability to understand that."

He smiled for the first time. "Oh, I understand all right. You want the absolute impossiblest thing in the world. No one can give you that promise, and if they did they'd be lying through their teeth."

"'Impossiblest' is not a word."

"Life after wife isn't a possibility." His tone hung in the air like frost even though it was over a hundred degrees outside.

"That's what I've been telling you, moron. I'm not mar- rying again ever." She accentuated each word with a poke of her fork toward him.

"Ever?"

She ignored the one word question.

"You going to answer?" Elijah asked.

"I was thinking about Kate. Get Hart to tell you how they got together. She said never ever, and it came back around to bite her on the fanny. I was just trying to be sure that I meant it, and I really do. So there, Elijah Jones."

"Tell me about Hart and Kate," Elijah said.

"Not me. No, sir. You want to know how they got together, you ask Hart. I already know. You ready to look at the rest of the books?"

CHAPTER FOUR

"Don't start without me," Kate yelled at the door.

Fancy grabbed her arm and hurried her to the kitchen where Sophie sat at the bar with a glass of tea in her hand. "There're cookies that Dessa made before she left on Friday. Tina is taking a nap, and Theron is at the church with the preacher interviewing a new youth minister. Sophie wouldn't say a word until you got here, and I'm dyin' to hear. Your tea is already poured, so sit down."

Kate downed half the glass of tea, picked up a cookie, and bit off a healthy chunk. "Dessa is a godsend. Don't ever let Theron fire her."

"Dessa isn't going anywhere." Fancy looked at Sophie. "OK, now tell us what happened since the funeral."

Kate picked up another cookie and turned around to face Sophie too. "Shoot," she said.

"Nothing much. Just the expected. He made this big to-do about getting up early and making a lot of noise, so if I didn't like it, I could sell out to him right then. So the next morning I was up and had breakfast ready before he even crawled out of bed. I hope it shocked the dickens out of him, because it wasn't easy getting up at four thirty or lying about it either," Sophie said.

Kate giggled and her pecan-colored eyes lit up. She wore cut-off jean shorts that were frayed at the hems and stopped mid-thigh. A bright orange tank top stretched over her frame like a second skin, and her black hair was pulled up with a big plastic clip.

"I told you that she'd get ahead of him on the first rattle out of the bucket," Fancy said.

She was almost five feet tall and eight months pregnant. Her pale blue maternity top was stretched out to the last thread. She had clipped her blonde hair up to keep it from sticking to her neck. She had blue eyes, but they weren't the same color as Elijah's. Fancy's had the warmth of a summer sky. Elijah's had the chill of a mountaintop capped with a layer of snow.

To take her mind off Elijah, Sophie reached out and touched Fancy's stomach about the time the baby kicked. "She wants out of there. Why don't you have her early?"

"Believe me, I would if I could. The doctor says if she's not here in two weeks he's going to induce labor," Fancy said.

"You absolutely sure it's a girl?"

"Looked like it on the ultrasound. Lord help us if it's not. Tina is expecting a sister. She might toss a brother in the trash can," Fancy said.

"If it's a mistake and a boy after all, I'll take Tina," Sophie said. "I can raise her as my own and not have to worry with a man."

"I don't think so," Fancy singsonged.

"And besides all that, you are changing the subject, and you don't get to do that. Is that tall, good-lookin' Native American goin' to be your life after wife?" Kate asked.

"That would not be a no, but a you've-got-to-be-nuts no! He's egotistical, too old, set in his ways, used to being top dog on the porch, and…" She searched for other horrible qualities.

"Too old?" Fancy frowned.

"He's forty. That's old," Sophie answered.

"That's not much older than you are. When you were ten and he was nineteen, it would have been. When you were twenty-one and he was thirty, it wouldn't have been so bad. But thirty-one and forty. That's nothing," Kate said.

"And you are almost thirty-two, so it's only eight years and some months," Fancy reminded her.

"It's closer to nine years, and I don't know when his birthday is so it could be a full nine years," Sophie argued.

"Well, if he's not your life after wife, then what is he?" Kate kept on.

"He's my business partner right now. We are just barely settling into the idea of sharing a house and a ranch. I'm seriously considering giving him the ranch house and buying myself a trailer and putting it on the back corner of the ranch. The only reason I don't is it would be giving him a point, and I'm determined not to lose even one. Give him the old proverbial inch, and he's liable to take a mile," she said.

Kate set the entire platter of cookies in the middle of the table. "Fancy, sit down and prop up your feet on this chair. You're goin' to drop that baby right here on the kitchen floor if you keep standin' up."

Fancy eased down into a chair and slung her legs up on the extra chair. "That does feel better, but if she'd fall out that easy, I'd stand up until dark."

"OK, now go on, Sophie. Who cares if he gets one point? If you put a trailer on the property, he'll know for sure that he's not running you off. And you won't be tempted to cook for him or clean up the house after him. He'd be on his own in that place, and you could take care of yours however you want to. Now that would be real business partners," Kate said.

"I agree," Fancy said. "Get a double-wide with all the bells and whistles. Front porch. Back deck. Or better yet, build a house. A great big one that makes his place look small. Talk about an ego buster."

Sophie ate three cookies while she listened and thought about such a venture. "I like it. Only I don't want a big house. I had that with Matt. I like the idea of a double-wide, so it could be ready to move into sooner. After the cattle sale, do you two want to shop with me?"

Fancy nodded and did the calculations in her head. "Three weeks until the sale. Baby should be here, and hopefully I'll be able to walk without waddling. Yes, I want to shop for your trailer with you."

Sophie looked at Kate. "How about you?"

"I'm in. You should do it. You've got the money, and if he's not going to be your life after wife, then you should get out of the same abode as he's in. No decent prospect is going to want to come courtin' if he has to go through the chief first," she said.

It started out as a schoolgirl giggle, with Sophie's hand going to her mouth. It went from that to a high-pitched laugh that sounded like it could crack crystal, and went into an infectious roar that had Kate and Fancy both wiping at their eyes and woke Tina from her nap down the hallway.

Tina snuggled down into what was left of Fancy's lap. She wrapped her arms around the baby bump and laid her head on the top. Fancy brushed her dark hair back out of her sleepy face. "Aren't you going to speak to the ladies?"

"Hi, Kate. Hi, Sophie," she mumbled. "What's funny?"

Sophie chuckled again. "Kate called Elijah chief."

"Why?" Tina raised her head up and knuckled her eyes.

"Because he's an Indian," Kate said.

Tina was suddenly wide-awake and interested. "You mean like on television? Does he live in a tepee?"

"No, he's just got Native American blood or Indian blood in him. Like you have Mexican blood," Fancy explained.

"Can I call him chief?" Tina asked.

"I don't think you should. He said you should call him Eli," Fancy said.

"I like chief better. It sounds like a dog. Can I name one of the kittens out under the porch, chief?"

"Yes, you can. That yellow one. He's got attitude," Sophie said.

"What's allitude?" Tina asked.

"It's what that yellow kitten has. Like when he walks all sideways and puffed up and then jumps on his brother. That's attitude," Sophie said.

"OK, then my lellow cat is Chief. I'm goin' to go find him and tell him. Momma, does Eli walk all sideways and jump out to scare Sophie?" Tina jumped down and ran out the back door before Fancy could answer.

"So tell me, why did me calling him chief set you off into a fit of laughter?" Kate asked.

Sophie downed half a glass of iced tea before she answered. "We had this big argument when I called him chief. He doesn't like to be teased about his heritage any more than I do about my Irish heritage. So we came to an understanding real quick. Now that's enough about me and my business partner."

"But not about you and your love life. When are you going to start dating? It's been almost two years. We've all been back in the area a year now, and Kate and I have already gotten our three magic words to come true. You haven't even made an effort. It's time, or else you're goin' to be an old, crazy ranch woman who hates men," Fancy said.

"What's so bad about that?" Sophie asked.

"You've got six months to get things straightened out. This is August. If you haven't been on a date by New Year's, then me and Fancy get to fix you up. You can go with me to the Ducaine family reunion. There's always good-lookin' cowboys at it," Kate said.

"I can find my own dates when I'm ready," Sophie protested.

"New Year's and then we're parading them through here at the rate of two every weekend. I get to pick one for Friday night, and Kate comes up with a Saturday date. Then on Sunday we'll have a full report. Conversation, food, and whether they were good kissers," Fancy told her.

Sophie's eyes widened. "You wouldn't!"

"Oh, honey, we definitely would," Kate giggled.

❖ ❖ ❖

Normally Elijah loved what quiet and solitude he could carve out of a day. But that Sunday afternoon, the silence was deafening. He roamed from one room to the other, sat on the deck, and watched the cows grazing beyond the yard fence. He ate a bowl of ice cream topped with chocolate syrup and pecans.

Finally, he got into his truck and drove five miles south into Baird. He'd thought about a cycle ride, but the heat was even more oppressive than it had been the day of Maud's funeral. Baird was an old cattle-drive town built back during the late 1800s. The three-block main street in town dead-ended at the railroad depot, which had been rebuilt in the last few years.

Elijah turned and drove slowly down the length of the place, looking at the buildings. What started out as thriving businesses had dried up one by one and sat empty, until a few antique stores breathed some life back into the town. Just like he remembered, the street was very wide with diagonal parking on either side.

He wished that the old, restored 1911 Texas & Pacific Railroad Depot was open, so he could spend an hour or so looking around in the museum located there. Maybe take a trip through the gift store or browse through the brochures in the visitor center. But it was closed on Sunday.

He parked out front and rolled down the window for a better look at the place. Heat rushed inside and sucked the air right out of his lungs. He pushed the button and rolled the window back up in a hurry. The flag out front hung limp. There wasn't a whisper of a breeze that hot August day, but then that was normal central Texas weather. Uncle Jesse said the wind blew every day until June first. Then it stopped, and you couldn't beg, borrow, buy, or steal a breeze until after Labor Day. Elijah smiled at the memory of Jesse sitting on the porch with a glass of sweet tea and saying those words.

He turned the Ford truck around and drove it back through town, past the courthouse, and on to the Dairy Queen. He parked out front and hurried inside, appreciating the cold air that greeted him. It was hot enough that he'd broken a sweat walking across twenty feet of parking lot. He ordered a large Dr Pepper and a hot fudge sundae and looked around for a place to sit.

"Hey, Eli, what're you doin' out in this heat?" Hart Ducaine called from a corner booth. "Bring that on over here and sit with me."

Elijah carried his sundae in one hand and the drink in the other and made his way to the booth. "What are *you* doin' out in the heat?" he asked Hart.

"Same thing you are probably. Got work that I could do, but it's hot and it's Sunday, so I can use that for an excuse not to do it. Got bored at home so I went for a drive and wound up down here. Thought I might drop by your place and get a preview of whatever cattle you might be thinkin' about sellin' at the sale next month. That way I'd know ahead of time if I could outbid that Australian feller that's been comin' around the last few years."

Eli dipped into the sundae. "You want something to eat?"

"No, I done already had a banana split and a Coke."

"Let me finish this and we'll go on out to the ranch, and you can take a look at the cattle. I haven't decided yet which ones will go to the sale. Sophie has to agree, and that's a helluva problem," he said.

Hart grinned. Like Elijah, he was over six feet tall. He had blond hair and light green eyes, and wore faded jeans and a T-shirt with a picture of a bull on the front. He'd followed the Pro Rodeo circuit for several years and won enough money to keep his ranch afloat for many years ahead. He and Kate had married in the spring, and from the get-go she'd insisted that Sunday afternoons belonged to her and her two friends. Most of the time, he didn't mind when there was a rodeo on television or even football or basketball. But that day the house was silent as a tomb.

"What are you grinnin' about?" Eli asked.

"Those women. Sophie givin' you a hard time, is she?"

"Worse than a hard time," Eli admitted.

"That's the way Kate was in the beginning," Hart said.

"That reminds me. Sophie said what's said in their witches' meetings is confidential. She told me a little about the way y'all got together, but she said I should ask you about the rest."

"What'd she tell you?"

"Not much. Just that you were her knight in shining armor."

"Not armor. I'm her knight in shining whatever, because she forgot the word 'armor' the first time she said it."

"And Theron is Fancy's forever thing, right?"

Hart chuckled down deep in his broad chest. "Yes, he is but he can tell you that story. Kate and I have a history going back to when we were kids. We went to school together over in Albany. She was a couple of years behind me, and I didn't notice her until my senior year. By then I was tied up with Stephanie, the head cheerleader. After graduation, Steph and I broke up, and I ran into Kate on the playground one night. We started seeing each other on the sly. I was scared to death of her father, so I didn't ask her out on a real date. Anyway, she got it in her head that I was sneaking around with her because I didn't want to be seen with a half Mexican. We broke up when Stephanie came cryin' back to me. That was my first big mistake. I was young and stupid and ignorant."

"Weren't we all?" Eli nodded.

"So anyway, after we broke up, I went to college and she moved away. Stephanie and I lasted a few weeks before the final split. When I came home for fall break, Kate was gone. I looked for her everywhere I went when I started bull riding professionally but never found her. Then Theron and Fancy got married, and I went to the reception. But back up. First I got this call from Stephanie, after more than a decade. She said she was in trouble and needed to talk to me. So I went to her motel room."

Eli raised an eyebrow.

Hart threw up a hand and shook his head at the same time. "Left fingerprints everywhere, but nothing happened between us. Anyway, I gave her my best advice, which was to call the cops and tell them her sad tale of woe, and went on to the wedding reception. Kate was there as maid of honor and dressed in this red satin dress that just took my breath away. I asked her who she was, and that made her mad enough to almost knock me on my ass. But in my defense, I was afraid to hope that she was really Kate Miller. So we danced and that led to having a drink, which led to the motel where we sat up half the night talking. She slipped out the next morn-ing, and I thought it was her knocking on the door because she forgot her key. Imagine my surprise when there stood two policemen with handcuffs and guns and a warrant for my arrest for murder."

"You are kidding me!" Eli scraped the bottom of the plastic sundae cup.

"Not a bit. They found my prints all over that motel room, along with Steph's dead body. I couldn't tell them that Kate was with me, since she was a relief police officer and trying to work her way into a full-time job. She was a crackerjack detective down in New Iberia, Louisiana. They hated to see her leave down there and tried to talk her into coming back when she'd been gone about six months. Anyway, it wouldn't look good if she was my alibi or that she had spent the night with me in a motel. We only talked that night, honest to God, but small towns have their own moral standards. Anyway, she didn't give me a choice. She stepped right up to the plate and told them she'd spent the night with me at the Ridge Motel."

Eli cocked his head to one side. "Then you had to make an honest woman out of her, right?"

"Lord, no. She wouldn't have a thing to do with me. Took me three months to talk her into marryin' me. She wouldn't believe that I'd been in love with her since we were kids. It got so bad that her grandma down in Louisiana had us both kidnapped and thrown out on an island in the swamp for a few days, so we'd have to either kiss or kill each other."

A slow, lazy grin lit up Eli's face. "I guess it's pretty evident that you didn't kill each other."

"So that's the story. I got down on one knee in her aunt's restaurant over in Kensington, in front of all the family and friends I could talk into being there that day, and proposed right there in public in front of everyone and her momma."

"A knight in shining whatever," Eli said.

"You got it! If she wanted a whatever, then by damn, I'd give her a whatever. I had a shirt made with this big WHATEVER done in silver on the front. That way I was her knight in shining whatever for sure."

"Romantic devil, ain't you?" Eli teased.

"I'd have proposed naked as a jaybird under the red light beside the courthouse to get that woman. I never chased after anything so hard in my life. It was about to drive me crazy," Hart said. "And if you ever tell her that, there will be a war between the white man and Indian man that will make Custer's last stand look like a Girl Scout picnic."

"Be careful there, white boy. You might wind up like Custer."

"Maybe so, but if she ever found out that bit of information, I'd probably be better off dead." Hart laughed.

"I'm glad I came to town today. Want to go out to the ranch now and see the cattle?" Eli changed the subject.

"Sure. I'll follow you in my truck. You and Sophie fight most of the time, huh?"

"Not most of the time. All of the time," Eli said as they walked out together.

Hart clapped him on the shoulder. "It'll get better."

"I'm not so sure I want it to. I'd just as soon she stay mad at me. Maybe then she'll decide that she can't live in the same house I do and sell me her half of the ranch," Eli said.

"Keep dreaming. That ranch is like a Texan's gun to Sophie. It's what kept her sane after her rascal of a husband died. The only way you'll get that ranch out of her hands is to pry it out of her cold dead fingers," Hart said seriously.

Sophie nosed her truck close to the fence, got out, and slammed the door. She didn't waste a lot of time getting from the truck into the house. If she was going to buy refrigerated air, then by golly she would enjoy it.

She smelled something good in the kitchen and followed her nose. Elijah was standing in front of the stove, stirring a pot of red sauce. He didn't even look up when she sniffed the air.

"What is that?" she asked.

"My famous spaghetti sauce."

"Is that supper?"

"It's *my* supper. Don't know what you are having," he said.

"You're not sharing?" she asked.

"Nope."

"OK then, but remember it works both ways. What's good for the goose is also good for the gander."

She picked a bibbed apron from the hook beside the door and tied it around her neck. Then she went to work. In half an hour, with very little effort, she had bread dough doing a fast rise in the warm oven and a lasagna ready to bake. She removed the dough, turned the oven up to 350 degrees, and flopped the dough out onto a flour-covered cabinet as far away from Elijah as she could get. She quickly made it up into a dozen yeasty rolls and rolled the remaining dough out onto the cabinet until it was a little more than an inch thick and oblong in shape. She cut up a whole stick of butter on top of that, setting the pats just right, and covered them with brown sugar and cinnamon. In a few more minutes, there was a pan of fresh cinnamon rolls on the back of the stove rising for the final baking step.

Elijah pretended he didn't care and didn't even know what she was preparing, but the first waft of that bread dough sitting near the warm oven made his mouth water. He dearly loved home-baked bread, and cinnamon rolls were his favorite dessert. But he would eat sawdust and wash it down with sewer water before he admitted that to her.

He boiled spaghetti and continued to stir his sauce.

She picked up one of those fat romance books with a woman draped over a bed and a bare-chested man merely inches from her lips pictured on the front. She propped her legs up on a chair and read while she waited for the lasagna to cook.

He'd tried to watch what she whipped up to go in her dish but had almost burned his sauce, so he didn't see what she'd added to the cream cheese, sour cream, and cottage cheese for the third layer. She'd put down several spoons of a sauce she'd made in ten minutes by browning hamburger with onions and peppers and adding a jar of prepared spaghetti sauce. Then she'd layered lasagna noodles on top of that. Uncooked ones. He'd never seen it done that way and wondered what the finished product would taste like. After that it was the white mixture. He thought he heard her cracking eggs, but surely not.

The timer sounded loudly. He drained the spaghetti noodles and poured them into a dish. He loaded up a plate and topped them off with a healthy serving of the sauce and carried the whole thing to the den where he put it on a wooden folding tray. A trip back to the kitchen netted a Dr Pepper from the refrigerator.

She looked up when he walked past. "Where'd you get that?'

"Bought it."

"Where?"

"At the store?"

"When did you go to the store? I had a list started of things we need for the house," she said.

"You need something. You pick it up. I needed Dr Pepper."

"Be careful there…" She bit back the word "chief" before it was out in the room. "I bought the last toilet paper. I could take it all to my bedroom and carry a roll with me to the bathroom. I don't have to share it."

"I don't plan to go into your bathroom. You stay out of mine. I'll buy my own paper."

"Good. I'll be nice enough to leave what's left on the roll for you. After that don't you dare steal a single roll out of my bathroom. Better get to that famous spaghetti. It's going to get cold," she said.

It took a healthy dose of his willpower to let her have the last word, but he managed to do it without choking on the unsaid words. He ate slowly and enjoyed every bite. When he finished, he washed his dishes, put the sauce in jars, stored them in the refrigerator for later, and meandered out the back door as slowly as he could.

She watched from the kitchen window and waited until he was halfway to the barn before she took out a jar of his sauce and dipped a spoon into it.

When it hit her mouth she moaned. "Mercy, that's the best sauce I've ever eaten. Why does he have to be such a rat and not share with me?" She ate two more bites and then put the lid on the jar with a long sigh.

Her bread turned out perfect. Light. Fluffy. Browned to perfection. She buttered the tops and turned the cinnamon rolls upside down on a serving tray before topping them off with a thin butter cream glaze. Then she turned on every ceiling fan in the house and opened his bedroom door. If he hated yeast dough, he'd have to live with the odor. If he loved it, she hoped he couldn't think about anything else.

She cut up a salad and dished up a healthy plate full of lasagna, added a roll on the side and a cinnamon roll on a separate plate, and carried it all out to the deck. The sun was setting, and the temperature had dropped a few degrees since she'd come back from Fancy's place.

Elijah was sitting in the hayloft, back in the shadows, when he saw her come out of the house. He quickly shimmied down the ladder into the barn and headed toward the house.

"What are you going to do?" she asked.

"Watch *60 Minutes*, a little *Sunday Night Football,* and then *Cold Case* at nine o'clock," he said.

"I watch *Desperate Housewives* at nine," she said.

"The big screen has *Cold Case* on at that time. You want to watch anything else, you do it in your part of the house," he told her.

"Anyone ever tell you what a mean old rat you are?"

"One time. I broke his nose. Anyone ever tell you what a witch you are?"

"Twice. They haven't found their bodies yet."

He shrugged and went into the house, where he carefully removed a cinnamon roll from the platter and shoved all the others up to fill in the space. He put it on a paper towel and carried it to his room. He locked the door and sat cross-legged in the middle of the bed while he ate it slowly, relishing every single bite. When he finished, he licked the remainder of the brown sugary goo off the napkin and from his fingers, not wasting a bit of it.

CHAPTER FIVE

"I promise I will be there for you just like you've been for me." Fancy managed to flash Sophie a weak smile after the delivery of her six-pound baby girl.

"You can be there for Kate, not me. It looked like too much pain for me," Sophie said.

Kate giggled. "I'll come collect your word, Fancy Lynn, and I'm not going to be nice and deliver at supper time. I'm going to do it at three in the morning. You're going to have to pay with interest. I want them two at a time so that I can catch up. Besides I'm tougher than either of you."

They were all gathered around Fancy's hospital bed. Theron's smile was bigger than anyone's as he squatted down to show Tina the new baby.

Hart stuck his head in the door. "Room for one more?"

"Sure. Come and meet Emma-Gwen," Theron said.

"Emma-Gwen?" Sophie frowned. "I thought you were naming her something weird, like Fancy or Echo."

"That's my name," Tina said. "Echo Martina is my name. New baby can't have my name."

Fancy winked. "Her full name is Glory Emma-Gwen, with a hyphen between the Emma and Gwen. Tina and I may still call her Glory."

"Her name is Emma-Gwen," Theron protested.

Tears welled up in Fancy's big blue eyes. "Does all that name sound like something you cure with penicillin? We haven't made the birth certificate yet. Does Glory sound too weird?"

Sophie bent over the bed and hugged her. "Of course it doesn't. Matter of fact, I like it very much. It sounds like the name for a woman president or Nobel Prize winner."

"Thank you," Theron mouthed silently from across the room.

Kate gave her a hug and grabbed Hart's hand. "Now that our job as cheerleading crew is over, I think we're going to get out of here and go home. Get some rest and call us. We'll visit as soon as you get back to the ranch."

"When are we buying her a pony?" Hart asked Theron as Kate pulled him out into the hallway.

"It's already in the stall," Theron answered before the door is shut.

"I'm going, too. You need to rest and some family time," Sophie said.

"Thank you for being here with us," Theron said.

"Hey, we were just the cheerleaders. You and Fancy did the hard work after we left you in here alone," Sophie told him.

"You know what we mean," Fancy squeezed her hand. "And since she was born on Sunday, we didn't miss our gab fest. I'll expect the same from you and Kate!"

"Kate, darlin'! Not me! She's the one tougher'n John Wayne. I'm the pansy. I'd be standing up in the stirrups screamin' at them to bring me more drugs," Sophie said as she left.

Sophie sat in her truck for five minutes before starting it. She'd laughed and teased about what Fancy had just endured, but she'd do it ten times over for a daughter like Emma-Gwen, and that's what she intended to call her. The new baby looked like an Emma-Gwen, not a Glory.

Elijah was snoring in the recliner while someone made a touchdown on the television when she walked into the house. He roused up when he heard the front door open and opened one eye enough to see that it was Sophie and not a terrorist or burglar.

"What'd she have?" he asked.

"A six-pound baby girl that they named Glory Emma-Gwen." Sophie sunk down into the corner of the sofa.

"That ain't even big enough for fish bait, and what kind of name is that? Sounds like something you need antibiotics for," he said.

"My Irish granny said that a woman could have them little, and they could grow big. They don't have to start out at ten pounds. And the name is their choice. Theron says they're goin' to call her Emma-Gwen. Tina's full name is Echo Martina, and Fancy's real name is Fancy. It's not a nickname. If she wants to name her child Glory, that's her business. It's not a bit worse than Elijah."

"Hey now, don't be attacking me. I just spoke my mind, and besides, Elijah is a good, solid name right out of the Bible. It was my great-grandfather's name."

"Yeah, well, so is Mephibosheth, and I don't like it either. Gwen is Fancy's mother's name, and Emma was Theron's grandmother."

"But I'll bet you Glory didn't come from anywhere in the family. Are they going to dress her in stars and stripes?" Elijah purposely provoked her. The madder she got, the more she'd hate living with him.

Sophie cooled down enough to know she was being baited. "Of course. She's going to have blue eyes and blonde hair like Fancy. Don't you think she'll be so cute next Fourth of July, all dressed up in a little outfit with red and white stripes? You've got to hold her. She'll wrap a big, old fellow like you around her finger in no time flat."

"I doubt it. I don't like kids. They grow up to be eighteen or nineteen years old and think they know everything. I've had to train too many kids already," he said.

"Is that what you did in the military? Train irresponsible kids?"

"I did lots of things. That was just one of my many jobs," he said.

"And you really don't like kids?"

"I really don't."

"Ever thought about having some of your own, or do you have a few floating around out there with your strange blue eyes?" she asked.

He bristled. "My eyes are not strange. They're not so different from Fancy's, and you don't think hers are strange. I think you just made a sly, little racial slur."

"And I think you are full of cow patties. I asked if you have any children. Are you going to answer the question?" she asked.

"The answer is no, and I'm not having any, either," he said coldly.

"Want to hear a funny story? That's the same thing Theron Warren said less than a year ago, and now he has two kids."

Elijah pondered on that for a while, trying to figure out how Theron got a child that was already three years old in less than a year. Surely there was an adoption, but he couldn't let it alone. Worrying with it for a few minutes like a hound dog with a big soup bone, he finally asked, "How'd that happen?"

"He was married a few years back to Tina's mother, Maria. She divorced him but didn't tell him she was pregnant," Sophie explained.

Both of Elijah's eyebrows shot up.

"Turns out that Maria had the maternal instincts of a rock when the baby was born. She left Tina with her sister about ninety percent of the time. Three years later, she met a rich guy from California and decided to marry him, only he didn't want children."

Sophie headed toward the kitchen to make a sandwich.

Elijah's curiosity got the better of his will power to not ask questions and not care. "Go on."

"One night out of the clear blue sky—actually it wasn't clear blue because it was freezing drizzle and putting a layer of ice on everything in sight —she calls up Theron and says to meet her in Decatur to get the child, or she'll leave her in the airport bathroom."

"Holy crap, Sophie! A rock does have more maternal instincts than that for sure," Elijah muttered.

Sophie slathered two sides of wheat bread with mayonnaise and stacked three pieces of ham on one side, cheese and lettuce and tomatoes on the other. She slapped it together and put it on a paper plate with some chips and got a cold Pepsi from the fridge.

"So he went and got her?" Elijah asked.

"He and Fancy were past the point where they wanted to murder each other by that time in their relationship. You'll have to ask him all about that part later. Anyway he called

Fancy and asked her to go with him," Sophie said and then took a big bite of the sandwich.

Elijah wondered if he was losing his ability to read people. Why would Theron need someone to go with him? His first impression of the man was that, although he was short, he was a stand-up kind of guy and didn't need a woman to hide behind.

Sophie swallowed and took a long drink from the can. "I bet you are wondering why he asked Fancy to go with him when they could barely tolerate each other, aren't you?"

"It's your story. I'm just listenin'," Elijah said in a flat tone.

Sophie took another bite. He could wait for the rest. His face, set like flint or stone or some other organism that did not breathe or move, said he could care less what she was prattling about. But his eyes told a different story. He must have gotten those from his Uncle Jesse's side of the family, because they were definitely interested and wanted to know everything.

She chewed slowly and had a potato chip before she continued. "Well, Fancy had been helping him in the Sunday school class that he taught for preschoolers, and he knew she'd be good with a little girl who might be terrified that her mother had abandoned her."

Elijah didn't say a word, but he didn't shut his eyes and snore or turn his vision back to the television, either.

"That's why he asked her to go with him, and it's a good thing he did because a few months later Maria showed up and tried to take Tina back with her. It was all a power play for money. She wanted him to pay her to sign over the rights to his daughter, and he refused. But Fancy had been there when it all went down, so Theron had a witness."

"That Maria really is a rotten apple," Elijah said.

"Yep. The lawyers had all this documentation that said Tina's DNA proved she was Theron's. And Fancy had signed a statement saying that Maria had actually left the child alone before they even arrived to get her, which constituted abandonment. So Maria didn't have a leg to stand on," Sophie finished the story.

"They ever see her again?" Elijah asked.

"Not so far. Hopefully she's out there in California and will stay there and not make trouble. I live in fear she'll kidnap Tina just for money."

Elijah stretched and stood up, shaking the legs of his cotton pajama bottoms down when he did. Without a word, he went to the kitchen and heated up some gumbo soup straight out of the can.

Sophie finished her sandwich, threw away the paper plate, and washed her hands at the kitchen sink. When she turned around, Elijah was just inches behind her on his way to the silverware drawer to get a spoon. For a moment their gazes locked, gray eyes doing battle with clear blue ones, and for a single breathless second she thought he might lean forward and kiss her. But it passed with a heavy awkwardness that sent her to her room with a weak excuse that she thought she heard her cell phone, and him back to check the soup on the stove.

She slung herself on the bed, head at the wrong end, feet on the pillow shams, and stared at the ceiling. A fly crawled across it, and she tried to concentrate on it rather than the emotional upheaval in her chest. She'd actually wanted Elijah to kiss her. It was definitely time for her to start dating again if a kiss from him was inviting. After the sale, if she hadn't found someone interesting, she would tell Kate and Fancy to start the process of fixing her up with Friday night dates.

She heard the familiar ringtone for Kate's calls. She slung her legs over the side of the high bed, bailed off, and grabbed it on the fourth ring.

"Hello. I was just thinkin' about you, and then you called," she said breathlessly.

"What is going on?"

"Nothing. Not anything. I just told you," Sophie said.

"And you are talking too fast and too furious and something else is happening. 'Fess up," Kate said.

Sophie took a deep breath. No way was she admitting that she wanted Elijah to kiss her!

"Did you leave right after I did, from the hospital I mean?" Kate asked.

"Yes, I did, and why are you calling? Is something wrong on your end?"

"Did you talk to anyone on the way out or on the way home?" Kate ignored Sophie's questions and kept asking her own.

"No, I did not, and stop interrogating me. I didn't commit murder or rob a liquor store. You are a farm wife now, not a detective," Sophie reminded her, hoping to flip the conversation toward Kate and get herself out of the hot seat.

"Okay, we've established that you haven't talked to anyone since you left the hospital, so something has happened between you and Eli," Kate said.

"Nothing happened. I told him about how Tina came to live with Theron and Fancy, and he made fun of the baby's new name. We got into a bit of an argument about that, which ended with him saying he never ever wants kids, and then you called."

"I smell a half-truth, Sophia Lauren McSwain. I'll let Fancy get the rest out of you when she's up and around. Want to go shopping in the morning for something pink and pretty to take to Emma-Gwen tomorrow night? That's why I called," Kate said.

"I'd love to, but we've got a full day getting ready for the sale. We've got appointments with caterers and the decorating crew, and the buyers are arriving in three days for the preshow look-see," she said.

"I hear a whine. Tell you what: I'll buy something, and you can pay me half. We'll meet at Fancy's place at eight tomorrow evening with the Welcome Home, Baby banner. Theron says they'll release her after twenty-four hours. I figure she'll be home right after that."

"I'm not whining. I'd far rather go with you than spend the time with Elijah. Surely I'll be done in time to get away by evening to welcome Fancy and Emma-Gwen home, though."

"What happened between you and Eli?" Kate asked suddenly.

Sophie almost answered, but caught her answer before it left her mouth. "Nothing. I'll see you tomorrow night."

"Chicken. Did he kiss you finally?"

"No!"

"OK, anything less than that can wait until later," Kate said and hung up.

Sophie threw herself back on the bed and flipped on the television set on her dresser. *Desperate Housewives* was playing, but she couldn't keep her mind on the show. It kept flitting around the idea of dating.

She definitely would have to get her own place. She'd been looking around the ranch when they were out culling cattle for the sale and had decided on the far southern corner. It faced a section line road, which would make it easy for her to come and go, and she wouldn't have to build a road from the house back to the trailer. There was a nice grove of pecan trees and a pond not far back on the property. She'd already thought about which trees would have to be removed and which could stay for shade.

The trailer would be facing the pond and the back door toward the road. The deck would look toward the north and run the whole length of the trailer, so she could sit out there during three seasons of the year and watch the sunrise and set both.

And she could bring dates home without having to deal with Elijah Jones. Maybe that's what made him so argumentative. He'd been one of those military playboys who had a girl in every state and didn't think he could date with Sophie in the house.

Why he didn't just sell her his property and buy another ranch was a mystery. At that notion, she perked up. She thought about it for a while, then jumped out of bed and grabbed her laptop. In a few minutes, she'd found two ranches not far from Baird, up toward Albany, that were for sale. She'd up her previous offer to enough money that he could purchase either one of them. She marched out to the den to find it empty. She opened the back door and found Elijah sitting on the deck staring out into space.

"What're you doin' back out here? I thought I heard your girly show playin' when I went down the hall a while ago." He didn't look at her. That little episode in the kitchen had sent him into a thinking spin. He needed a woman in his life, and finding one at his age that didn't have a couple of divorces and teenage kids under her belt wouldn't be an easy job.

"I was piddling on the Internet and found a couple of ranches for sale within twenty miles of this one." She hoped her voice didn't sound too excited.

"So you lookin' to buy or sell?"

"Buy. But not for myself. The biggest one is up by Albany. I'll buy it and deed it over to you, if you'll give me your half of this ranch."

"Ain't happenin'. This has been Jones property since back before Baird was even put together. Uncle Jesse said he could prove it was Jones property back about the time that Sam Houston stomped Santa Anna's rear end and Texas became a state. So it's not going to be McSwain property now. You go buy that Albany ranch. It'd put you closer to your friends anyway," he said.

"Why don't you listen to reason? This is my ranch. I took care of Aunt Maud. I know this place. I love it. I'll even keep the brand and the name. It won't be McSwain property." She would have rather snatched his ponytail right off his head than kissed him.

"No, ma'am, it won't be. It's goin' to be mine, or at least half mine, until the day I die," he said.

"And then who will you leave it to? You don't have children that you are claiming, and you don't want any. You think it's going to stay Jones property after you are dead?" she asked.

"Don't know about that. But it will be while I'm living. All I can take care of is what I do with it in my lifetime. The next generation can pick up the responsibility from there.

I intend to do just what Uncle Jesse wanted me to do. Live here, run this ranch, and love it." Elijah was glad that he'd remembered to say Uncle Jesse rather than Aunt Maud. One of the stipulations she made in her last letter was that he never tell anyone that she left him the property. It had been broadcast among her friends and family that it had been Jesse who had willed him half the ranch.

Sophie went back into the house and let him have the last word. It was beginning to look more and more like she would have to share. But by golly, she did not have to like it or live in the same house with Elijah Jones. As soon as Fancy was able, they were going shopping for a double-wide.

CHAPTER SIX

Sophie wanted to rip up the plans laid out on the dining room table. They looked like blueprints for a presidential inauguration, rather than a cattle sale party held in a barn. She and Maud had simply met with the caterers who kept plans from year to year and tweaked them to fit with that year's ideas. According to Maud, not much had changed in the fifty years they'd had the ranch.

She stared at the five feet of paper rolled out and held down on all four corners with a steak knife. "Why did you go to all this trouble? Cleaning out the barn and getting things ready is a big chore, but the caterers bring everything else. The band sets up and we have a party. This was unnecessary."

"We're setting a precedent this year. Maud is gone. Buyers are going to be cautious until they figure out how we do things. We make a big splash at this year's sale and it'll keep the stock up, so to speak," he said.

She cut her eyes around to look at him. "Just exactly what did you do in the service? Was it air force or army or what?"

"Air force. I did many jobs. What has that got to do with this?"

"You remind me of...never mind."

"Small ranches like this one are quickly being swallowed up by the big corporations. If we want to stay alive, we have to put on a united front that says we are prosperous. Maud was solid as concrete. They don't know how you and I are going to run this operation together. If they smell a drop of blood, the bidding at the sale will be low. Coyotes always go after the wounded chicken," he said.

Sophie didn't feel like a wounded chicken at all. She was more alive than she'd ever been, but what he said made sense. "So these plans aren't the whole story. Spit out the rest of it."

"Truce. We have to call a truce and be business partners at least on the side that people see. No fighting in front of anyone. They have to think that we are settling into our halves so well that it's the same whole package that Maud gave them. Our brand is still reputable. They're buying from a prosperous little ranch, and we are running it together," he told her.

She sat down and really studied the party layout. It was all backward to what she and Maud had done, but it could work. The old girl would turn over in her grave if they had a bad sale the first year they were out of the chute. She'd given her energy and life for the ranch—fought mesquite, rattlesnakes, and coyotes; pulled calves; managed the finances; and loved it all. To let it slide into mediocrity because Sophie was too stubborn to listen to good common sense would be a shame.

"Tell me more," she said.

"We move out equipment today and clean the barn. Starting tomorrow morning, there will be a caterer out of Dallas here every day. They will set up a table and a bar in this corner." He pointed to the backside of the barn, away from the center where the cattle would be displayed one at a time for the auctioneer to sell.

"Why there?" she asked.

"Put it close to the door and the buyers might be tempted to sneak on outside after they've gotten a drink or a food tray," he explained.

"We didn't wine and dine them during the sale before," she said.

He sat down beside her. His face was serious, and there were no twinkles in his blue eyes. This was totally business. "They'll stay if they have food and drinks. This is as important as the after-party. A man gets hungry, he's going to find food, believe me. He'll leave and maybe he'll come back later, or maybe he'll just go on home and watch NASCAR on television. If he stays, he'll see a cow or a bull or a lot of calves that he wasn't really expecting to buy, but they'll look good. He'll bid and the man who really came to buy those calves will bid higher because he really wants them. It's all..." he looked for the right word.

"Manipulation," she finished it for him, not knowing whether she liked it or not.

"I'd say 'good business tactics.' Are we in agreement up to this point?"

She nodded, even if it did mean swallowing a heck of a lot of pride. "It's going to cost double what we paid for the sale last year."

"We'll make it back and more. Trust me."

Trust him!

Now that was an oxymoron. He was a man, wasn't he?

"The caterers will bring enough help during the days of the sale that they will circulate in the balcony with trays of drinks. Iced tea and lemonade. Drunk men don't keep their heads on for bidding."

"You got it all figured out, don't you?" she said through clenched teeth.

"Yes, I do," he said shortly.

"Don't snip at me. I'm not stupid. I understand your logic. Keep them in the balcony, and they'll buy more," she shot right back.

He ran his fingers through his shoulder-length, straight black hair. It still had water droplets clinging to it from his morning shower and smelled so good that Sophie had trouble keeping her mind on the party. The white gauze undershirt didn't hide a single bulging muscle. No, sir. It just clung to his well-defined abs like paint on a park bench.

"OK," he went on. "Three days of sales. Starting at ten in the morning. Stopping at three."

"We started at eight and went to five," she muttered.

"Let them sleep in and have a leisurely breakfast at their motels or in their campers. Stop in time that they can prowl around the antique shops with their wives and think about what's going on the bidding block the next day," he said.

It made sense, and she wondered why she and Maud hadn't thought about things like that. "Is that all?" she asked.

"Then, after the last bull is sold, we hire double the help to whip the sale barn into shape, and this is the layout for the party. White tablecloths, good food, and music that says thank you."

She waited several seconds to see if he was finished. "I insist on the same caterers for the party that we've always used. They will take care of the sale business much cheaper than anything out of Dallas. And they're big enough to have all those white tablecloths. Maud just never wanted to pay for that much."

"No problem. You already have an appointment with them?"

She was shocked speechless. "Yes, I do. They'll be here in an hour."

"Then I'll call the Dallas caterers and tell them to cancel their appointment for this afternoon. If the local one can do the job and keep business closer to home, that's good business," he said.

"That's what Maud said," she told him.

"Just one addition." He flipped open a book and looked at the menu from last year.

"And what's that?" Sophie asked.

"Steaks. Tell them we want a couple of big grills set up outside the back door of the barn so that the smoke won't get in the ladies' hair when they come inside. No one wants to smell like T-bone when they're dancing with a good-lookin' man." He made a notation on the side of the page.

"Why?"

"Because perfume and good-smellin' hair smells better to a man than steak when he's hugged up to a woman on the dance floor."

"Not that. Why steaks? They bring every kind of barbecue you can think of for the buffet," she said.

"Because of the smell of a grill. It drifts out across the pasture and yard and makes them hungry even before they step in the doors. They'll remember that for a long time, and it'll bring them back next year," he answered.

"You've thought about this a lot, haven't you?"

He shrugged. "I'm making this my home. I want to do well."

She remembered what Tandy had said at the lunch after the funeral. She'd been right—Elijah had come home, just like she had. No matter how mean or cantankerous she got, he wasn't leaving. That meant accepting the fact that she had a new business partner. It also meant she'd have to stay on her toes and be alert, or he'd gradually take over the ranch anyway, and she'd just be a name on the deed.

"Is that all?" she asked again.

"Just one more minor detail. We will stand united at the front door to greet each guest. It'll only take an hour or so and will say thank you in a special way. You got a problem with that?"

She shook her head. "We can't circulate among the buyers and friends if we are stuck at the front door, so yes, I do have a big problem with that."

"There will be plenty of time for circulating and talking to the people. After the first hour, we'll make the rounds together. And we'll meet each person for sure if we are at the door."

"That looks like we are a couple," she said.

"No, it looks like we are partners," he argued. "If we danced every dance together and I looked down into your eyes with 'I want to kiss you' written all over my face, that would make us a couple, God forbid."

She bristled. "Why 'God forbid'?"

"God forbid because there would be a murder. One of us would be dead. The other would be in jail, and the ranch would be sold on the auction block to some big corporation that would bulldoze the house down and grow wheat to send to a third-world country," he said.

"So what's my job in all this?" She ignored the statement about murder because it was the gospel truth and couldn't be added to or taken away from.

"Call in the crew to start cleaning. I suppose you and Gus have already discussed that, haven't you?" Elijah asked.

"Of course," she lied. "If that's the end of the conversation, I'm going out to the barn to take a look around. Unless you want to tell me how to fix my hair and what to wear to the shindig?"

He grinned.

She was amazed at how it softened his angular face. "What?"

"I reckon you'll wear jeans and a fancy shirt. After all, it's a western-type barn party, not a black-tie dinner at the Waldorf."

Had he been to such an affair? She wouldn't have asked, even if it meant the difference between visiting with Lucifer or the angels on Judgment Day, but suddenly she wanted to know more about the Elijah who wasn't a soldier, who wasn't as stubborn as a Missouri mule, and who was a very handsome, well-organized man.

He rolled up the plans.

She headed to the barn, hoping that Gus was there and he'd already hired help to start the cleanup process. If not, she was in big trouble with her new "partner." She made quote marks with her fingers before she put a hand on the yard fence and hopped over it with the agility of a cougar. She found Gus sitting in the smallest John Deere tractor about to start it up to move it out of the barn.

"Hey, Miz Sophie," he waved.

She motioned for him to get out of the cab and kept walking toward him, keeping an eye over her shoulder the whole time. Hopefully, Elijah was making his cancellation calls to the Dallas caterer or pretending to do so. She wouldn't put it past him to have never called one at all. That way he could concede a small point to her without losing anything he wanted.

"How many men we got coming for cleanup this afternoon?" she asked.

"Regular crew. I called them last week and set it up," Gus said.

"Can you get four or five more? Pay them extra if you have to. We're doing a little more this year. Caterers will be here the whole time starting tomorrow morning, and they need a place to set up earlier than the day after the sale."

Gus rubbed his chin. "Well, Rick's son would be glad for the work, and he's got a nephew that just got laid off over at the plant in Abilene, and I bet he'd know a few men who'd be glad for some extra work. Pay 'em in cash?"

"That's right, at the end of each day. See if they can come on in right after lunch. And you supervise when they get here. They can do the heavy stuff," she said.

Gus was a man of few words normally and didn't get into anyone's business. He'd been on the ranch for years and knew every square inch of it.

"Miz Sophie, who is my boss? You or Mr. Elijah? I ain't got no beef with either one of you, but I need to know who to listen to." He removed his old straw hat and ran his fingers through hair that had more gray than black. His face was a study in weathered wrinkles.

For the first time in all the years she'd known him, his eyes looked worried.

"We both are. If I tell you something and he says different, just come talk to me, and we'll work it out among the three of us. I tried to buy him out. I've tried to run him out. Nothing works, so I guess we are partners until one of us dies of pure old stubbornness," she said with a smile.

Gus slapped his old straw hat into shape and resettled it on his head. "How do you feel about that?"

"Don't matter how I feel. It's the way it is. He won't sell to me, and I ain't budgin'. Been thinkin' about putting a trailer on the back corner of the property. Back in that pecan grove," she said.

"Guess that's one way to deal with it," Gus said.

CHAPTER SEVEN

The actual cleaning began right after lunch.

The fighting began ten minutes after that, when the two chiefs disagreed on what the hired hands should do.

All the equipment had been moved outside: the ranch's two biggest John Deere tractors, two four-wheelers, and the company work truck. At that point Sophie figured they'd get out the four-foot brooms, sweep the joint out, make sure the cobwebs were knocked down, and call it a day.

She'd located half a dozen wide brooms and scanned the interior of the barn for spiders and scorpions. She saw a couple of bugs scoot off in search of a hidey-hole, but, after it was swept out, she'd bring out the foggers and that would take care of them. Tomorrow the hired hands would sweep up whatever dead varmints the fog had killed, and then they'd help round the cattle up into pens for the sale. She'd done this the year before, back when it was just a cattle sale and not a Broadway production.

She'd picked up a broom when she heard Elijah shout.

"It's here!" Elijah was as excited as a little boy on Christmas morning.

"What?" Sophie ran to the door and shaded her eyes with both her hands.

"The power washer. They said they'd deliver it right after lunch, and, by golly, they are right on time," Elijah said.

"Power washer?" Sophie asked.

Elijah nodded. "We could rent it for a hundred dollars or buy one for five hundred. Since we'll be using it every year, I bought it."

Both of Sophie's eyebrows tried to jump to the top of her brow. "You didn't consult with me."

"Nope."

"We are partners, Elijah. That means..."

He set his jaw and his blue eyes narrowed. "If I'd bought the thing with ranch money, I would have talked to you. I paid for it. It's my power washer. Does that make you feel better, Miz Queen of Sheba?"

"What on earth do you need a power washer for?" She ignored the barb and kept pace with him as he motioned the pickup truck to back up to the garage.

"To really clean this place out before the caterers come with their snow-white tablecloths," he said.

"Are you Elijah Jones?" A tall, blonde delivery girl crawled out of the truck. Denim shorts looked like they'd been spray-painted on her body; her shirt hugged every curve, leaving little to the imagination; big hoop earrings touched her shoulders and drew the eye away from her short spiky hair. Her eyes were brown, and the way they scanned Elijah from boots to ponytail, evidently she liked what she saw.

"Yes, I am," Elijah said.

Pure old jealousy shot through Sophie's heart like cupid's famous arrow.

"It's five hundred forty-nine dollars and sixty-nine cents plus twenty dollars for delivery. I was told you'd have a check ready for me," the woman said.

"Follow me. The business checkbook is in the house. Gus, holler at a couple of the men to come get this off her truck," Sophie yelled over her shoulder.

Elijah took two steps toward Sophie and looked down into her eyes. "I said I was paying for the thing."

"And I say the business is paying for it. You leave; it stays. I might want to spray something else with it after you're gone." She did not blink.

"I'm not going anywhere, darlin'." He drew the last word out into five syllables and made it sound downright mean.

"Neither am I, except to the house to write this woman a check," she said.

Gus brought two men from the barn, and they all three leaned on the truck, staring at the apparatus. Gus removed his straw hat and wiped the sweat from his forehead. "Looks like it'll have some power. Never thought of using one of them things to wash things down. I betcha it'll do the work in half the time, but I hear they make your arms pretty darn sore."

Elijah walked away from Sophie without another word and joined the men at the truck. Sophie motioned for the woman to follow her and stomped toward the ranch house, the dirt billowing up behind her cowboy boots.

The woman had to hurry to catch up and was out of breath when they reached the house. Sophie opened the back door and stood to one side to let her enter first.

"Would you like a glass of iced tea or a soda? There's Pepsi and Dr Pepper," Sophie asked.

"Dr Pepper, please. It's too hot to run," she sputtered.

Sophie grinned as she removed one of Elijah's sodas and handed it to the girl. "Honey, that wasn't even jogging. That was just a good old, angry fast-walk."

"Well, I live in air conditioning, work in it, and even when they talk me into a delivery, I ride in it. And to top it all off, I work out in a gym that is air-conditioned. I do not run in the heat," she said.

"Oh, I thought you were here to use the power washer. At least give us a demonstration," Sophie said.

The girl gulped down several drinks of the cold soda pop before answering. "No, ma'am! Not me. I've seen the guys at work use one of those things. It'll wear you plumb out in a hurry. Let your husband do the washin', honey. You just stand back and tell him what a good job he's done."

Sophie almost choked. "He's not my husband!"

The girl grinned. "Your significant other?"

"No!" Sophie filled a glass with water and drank deeply.

"Then if he's fair game, I might ask him out. How old is he?"

Sophie set the glass down so hard that the remaining water sloshed out on the cabinet. Why did she care if the woman asked Elijah out for ice cream or to dinner?

You've been talking about getting back into the dating game and moving a trailer out on the backside of the property so that Elijah wouldn't know who you went out with and when, so why the sudden green streak in your heart? That niggling little voice inside her head wouldn't hush.

"How old are you?" Sophie finally asked.

"Nineteen," she said with a brilliant smile.

"Then, honey, he's old enough to be your father," Sophie answered. "Office is back here. Come on and bring that invoice so I can write your check."

"Really." The girl followed Sophie into the dining room and down the long hallway with doors opening on either side.

"He's forty," Sophie said.

"Well, dang it! I thought he might be about thirty, and that's my top limit," she said.

Sophie took the invoice from her hand and sat down behind the desk. She opened the business checkbook and wrote out the amount on the bill, tore it off, and handed it to the girl.

"What's your low limit?" she asked.

"Seventeen to thirty. No older. No younger. I might make an example with Elijah. I even like his name. Sounds like an old western. I bet he'd be a good dancer. Oh, well." She sighed. "Got to stay with my rules."

"Might be a good idea," Sophie said as she opened the back door.

Miz Blondie Rules sucked in air when the blast of heat hit her square in the face. "I'm going to the lake tonight. Put on my bikini and stay in the water until dark," she said.

"Have fun." Sophie led the way to the barn, remembering back when she was nineteen and had life all figured out. She'd find a wonderful man at college; they'd fall in love and live happily ever after.

Yeah, right! That only happens in the movies and romance books. So enjoy your youth, sweetheart. It will end, and reality will hit you between the eyes so hard it'll knock your socks off.

Elijah and the hired hands were in the barn, sweeping furiously with more dust blowing around them than was being swept away. The delivery gal waved at them, her Dr Pepper can high in the air, before she crawled up into the pickup and drove off.

Elijah threw his broom down and met Sophie at the door. "You gave her one of my Dr Peppers?"

"I did." Sophie smiled.

"Then you can replace it," he said.

"You would have given her one if you'd gone to the house to write her a check," Sophie argued.

"Yes, but that would have been different," he said.

"No, it would not. She would have still rode off with a can of soda pop in her hands," Sophie countered.

"You are splitting hairs," he said.

"You are being obstinate. The business paid for the power washer. You can pay for a can of soda pop," she said.

"It's not the money," he growled.

"Get over it." She brushed past him and picked up a broom to help sweep the barn floor free of hay, dirt, and feed remnants.

He grabbed his broom and kept up with the men on either side of him as they pushed the worst of the debris toward the back door. When that job was finished, he and Gus hooked up the power washer to the water well, and Elijah rolled up his shirtsleeves.

He stretched out enough hose to the washer to reach all the way to the balconies surrounding three sides of the barn and started on the south side. He motioned to Gus to turn it on and held on tightly. Still, the first blast almost knocked him flat on his rear end before he adjusted his hands to a firmer hold and started washing down the walls and seats in that area. Water poured down into the barn like hard rain and ran everyone out into the heat, slapping their straw hats against their pant legs to get the water off.

"Felt pretty good." Gus laughed. "He said to give him half an hour and send Kendall up there to relieve him. There's four of them all itchin' for a turn at the washer. I figure they'll all be cryin' the blues with sore muscles come mornin' time, but the old barn will look spiffy when they get done."

Sophie nodded. She'd seen the washer come close to whipping Elijah. She didn't want a thing to do with it. It would prove that she wasn't as big and strong as King Kong, and Elijah sure didn't need to know that.

"Well, I expect you all can handle this. I'm going to take a four-wheeler out to the pasture and take one more look at the cattle. It's my first year without Maud to tell me which ones to sell and which ones to keep," Sophie said.

Gus nodded but didn't take his eyes from the wash job going on up in the balcony. The sprayer washed years' worth of dirt and grime away from the seats, leaving behind wood that looked practically new. New ranch owners, a new way of doing things, a new look. Gus wondered if it was time for him to retire and let a younger man step up to the plate.

Elijah saw Sophie mount up on one of the four-wheelers and go roaring off in a cloud of dust toward the east. She'd be going out to check on the cattle they'd agreed to sell to make sure that there wasn't a single cow that she wanted to keep another year. He'd done the same thing early that morning and, after a close check, had decided that he'd leave the list alone. There was one Angus bull, a two-year-old that had a lot of promise, that he really had misgivings about selling. His bloodline was pure, and his father was the pride and joy of the ranch, but they didn't need another breeding bull right then. The young bull's father was still in good health and young enough to use for another five to six years. There would be more calves to come along in that time that would be replacement-breeding stock.

His thoughts left the bull and went straight to Sophie. She'd grown up from a gangly girl to a fine woman. He'd never been drawn to red-haired girls before, but there was something about that kinky red hair of hers that made him want to tangle his fingers in it to see if it was as soft as it looked.

"Whoa, boy!" he muttered. "She's your partner, and you'd ruin everything if you ever let your crazy heart go there."

But telling his heart to stay away and making it do so were two very different things. The forceful spray of water became a screen for pictures of Sophie. At the breakfast table with that gorgeous red hair all tied up in a ponytail, with strands wiggling their way out of the rubber band like disobedient children; cleaned up and smelling like springtime flowers as she picked up her purse and went off to one of her Sunday things with the girls; the love in her foggy gray eyes when she looked at Fancy Lynn and Theron's new baby daughter; the fire in those eyes when they argued.

He was deep into the visions when Kendall tapped him on the shoulder and turned off the machinery. Elijah jumped and went into defensive military mode, catching himself just before he shot a fist out and decked Kendall.

"Sorry, man, you startled me," Elijah said softly, the silence in the barn even more deafening than the loud power washer.

"I should've turned off the machine first," Kendall said. "Didn't think of it until I saw the look in your eyes. Scared me."

"Sorry," Elijah said again.

"No problem. Sure looks good where you've been." Kendall nodded toward the seats and walls that were already drying in the hot wind blowing through the barn.

"I thought it would. We'll finish up here and then work our way down the walls inside, ending with the floor. Then we'll shut the doors. It'll be hot but it'll keep the tumbleweeds and dirt from blowing right back inside," Elijah explained.

He flexed his arms and rolled his shoulders. "I'll be back in an hour or so for another turn. Hang on tight. It'll give you a workout."

Kendall was a tall, lanky boy with a crop of blond hair that needed cutting and dark green eyes. He nodded and grabbed the hose with both hands. "I ride bulls on the weekends so I'm used to a workout. Let 'er rip, partner!"

Elijah grinned and flipped the switch.

Kendall laughed and yelled, "Whoa, hoss! You are a mean one, ain't you?"

Elijah made his way down the steps and out into the yard where Gus was directing the hired hands toward the two riding lawn mowers. "I told them to mow the yard and the lawn, then at least a hundred yards around the barn. They'll be parking their trucks over on the north side, so get a good wide swath cut over there, too. That about right, Elijah?"

"Sounds like you got it under control. Miz Sophie go to check on the cattle one more time?" Elijah asked.

Gus nodded.

"Think I'll join her. Tomorrow things will be going pretty fast, and this might be our last time to make absolute sure what we want to sell off. Oh, and I offered for Theron and Hart to bring over a few of theirs to make our sale bigger. They do their sales in the spring, and we can take a few of ours to theirs. So they'll be bringing theirs to the pens sometime in the morning."

"Miz Maud did that some in the past, especially when her sale wasn't going to be a big one. Y'all bein' cautious this year?" Gus asked.

"Not really. We're culling out pretty good, and then we plan to restock with some new blood," Elijah told him.

"I think that's a good thing. Maud, she got attached to the cows and didn't want to sell off what she should. Sophie will do the same if you don't keep on your toes. She's like Maud. Hard as nails on the outside but softhearted," Gus said.

Elijah chuckled. "I ain't seen none of that soft part yet."

"Nope, you ain't, but you might. We'll be right here mowin' and then rakin'. That'll take most of today, and then tomorrow the folks with the tables and all will come, right?"

"That's about it. Tell Randy that he's up next on the washing business, and Taylor can have the next turn after him. I'll be back by that time and take over. It should be pretty well done by then." Elijah mounted the second four-wheeler and rode off in the direction that Sophie had gone.

He found her sitting under a pecan tree in the shade, studying the cows grazing near a farm pond. Some were wading out into the muck surrounding the water that was evaporating too fast in the sun's blistering heat. Some were chomping at the green grass, and some were lying down chewing their cud as contentedly as if there were no steaming heat waves rising from the water.

He stopped and dismounted like he was getting off a horse.

"Any changes?" he asked.

"No, and you didn't have to come check on me."

"I'm not. I wanted to take one more look. We'll round them up tomorrow and get Randy and Kendall to hose them down."

"You sure you don't want to hire a hairdresser to come braid ribbons into their tails?" she asked sarcastically.

He gritted his teeth. "Stop fighting me on every issue. Big spenders like pretty stock. Hose the mud off and those cows will bring another hundred a head. Multiply that by…"

"OK, OK!" she said. "It's just different than what Aunt Maud did. I wasn't prepared to do it any different, and then you come along with all these ideas."

"I want this to work, Sophie. I want to live here, to make it a going concern. If washing down the barn and the cattle make us more money, then that's what we'll do."

She shut her notebook. "Truce then, until after the sale. When we add up the profits and compare them to last year's, we'll see if it was all worthwhile."

She stuck out her hand.

He reached across and shook.

Neither was prepared for the shocking tingles that glued their boots to the ground.

CHAPTER EIGHT

Sophie put a Sammy Kershaw CD in the player and picked up a romance book she'd checked out the last time she went to the library. She and Elijah had eaten soup from cans: she'd had gumbo, and he'd had some kind of beef stew. She'd sliced some Italian bread and toasted it with pepper jack cheese under the broiler, and opened a jar of peaches that she and Aunt Maud had canned the spring before.

After the jolt that had passed between them when they shook hands, neither had had much to say. They'd eaten, cleaned up their dishes, and Elijah mumbled something about a shower. She'd kicked off her boots, put on the music, and intended to read, but the words all blurred together as Sammy sang "Don't Go Near the Water."

"Too late," she mumbled. "I done went near the water and I can't swim."

What are you fussin' about? Aunt Maud's voice argued so close to her ear that she turned quickly to make sure the old girl hadn't resurrected and came to visit. No one was in the bedroom with her, but Aunt Maud continued. *You can swim just fine, girl. Now why are you hiding in your room? Ain't Elijah good company?*

"Listen to the song, Aunt Maud. Sammy is singing that he didn't go near the water, but he got his feet wet. That's the way I feel. I don't like Elijah, but I got jealous when he looked at the delivery girl, and when we shook hands, something jarred loose in my heart that I buried so deep it wasn't ever supposed to surface."

All she got was a soft chuckle and a soft breeze across her face in answer.

"I'm crazy!" she muttered. "I'm talkin' to the dead and imaginin' ghosts. See what a man in my house has done to me? Those boys in the white jackets and the unmarked van are going to appear in the front yard if I don't get it together."

The ringtone on her cell phone jerked her back to the present. She rolled to the other side of the bed and fetched it from the nightstand.

"Hello. I'm glad you called. I'm going crazy," Sophie said.

"You're about to go more crazy. Has anyone called you?" Kate asked.

Goose bumps as big as a herd of Angus bulls popped up on Sophie's arms. "What?"

"There's a wildfire to the southeast of you. I just heard about it. It's headed right for your ranch, lady. I'm surprised you hadn't heard already," Kate said.

Someone started beating on the front door so hard that the glass rattled. "Someone is here. I bet Gus heard and he's here. Thanks."

"Call if you need help," Kate said.

Sophie shoved her feet down in her boots and ran down the hallway toward the door. She slung it open to see Gus and three of the hired hands wearing worried expressions and motioned them inside. Before they were in the house, Elijah was in the room, smelling like soap and Stetson aftershave and wearing cotton pajama bottoms with a black T-shirt stretched across his broad chest.

"We'll get the cows up in the pens close to the barn," Gus said.

"What's happening?" Elijah asked.

"Wildfire. Started down southeast of us. It's bypassed Baird, but it's eating up farm land, and this wind is blowing it toward the ranch," Gus said.

"Firebreaks," Sophie said.

Elijah had to stop himself from tearing off his pajamas right there in the foyer. He headed down the hall and yelled over his shoulder, "I'll get dressed, and we'll plow firebreaks if you all can gather in the stock. Start in the south and herd them north toward the two barns. We've got pens ready for the sale. Put as many as you can in the pens."

"And the yard should hold at least thirty head so fill it up too," Sophie said. "I'll take the older tractor. I'm used to it, and I'll start a firebreak along the south fence line. You come in behind me, and we'll make it double-wide. Next year we're putting in metal posts if I have to finance them out of my personal account."

"I been tellin' Miz Maud that for years. One of these days the fires are going to burn up every one of them old wood posts," Gus said on his way out the door. "Frankie, you and Kendall go get on them four-wheelers. I'll drive my truck, and Randy can take the old work truck. I just hope we don't run too many pounds off them right here at sale time."

"Better to be ten pounds skinnier than burned right out there in the field," Sophie said as she took off in a dead run toward the barn. She quickly backed the tractor up to a wide plow, hooked it up, and took off for the southernmost field as fast as she could make the old girl go. The sun was a big old orange ball off to the west, but the southern wind carried the smell of smoke, and where there was smoke there would be fire right behind it. The breeze was scalding hot, but, in spite of it, cold chills danced down her spine. Was she about to lose the ranch right there at sale time? What would happen to the cattle? What if she lost a barn?

So many questions and not one dang answer.

Elijah wasn't far behind her, and they lowered their plows at the same time. She kept the front tires as close to the barbed wire fence as possible. He came along on her left, doubling the size of the firebreak. Even if it burned the posts and the fence fell, maybe the freshly plowed dirt would bring it to a halt. If the wind would just stop blowing, the firebreak would work for sure.

"Too many ifs," she mumbled and stole a glance over her shoulder. Elijah was doing a fine job, and with any luck the two of them would keep the fire from destroying their ranch.

"Our ranch," she said aloud. "Not mine, but ours. Sounds strange, Aunt Maud."

Dry, hot weather and brown pasture grass made perfect conditions for a Texas wildfire, and Aunt Maud had told her stories that would uncurl her red hair, but this was her first experience with one. The smoke snuck into the tractor cab through the air vents and made her cough, but she kept plowing, checking her rearview mirror frequently to make sure Elijah was still back there. They were almost to the end of the section line when she saw black smoke billowing across the rolling hills, red and yellow blazes as tall as a two-story house right behind the smoke. She stopped the tractor and watched as it surrounded the neighbor's oil-storage tank and gained even more momentum when the tank exploded in a loud roar.

Elijah caught up to her and hopped out of his tractor, slung open her door, and shouted above the constant noise of fire eating whatever lay in its pathway. "It's going to break and spread around us. I'm going back to the east to plow one width against the ranch line on that side. You take the west. Did you bring your phone in case you get into trouble?"

She shook her head. "Just go. If I get into trouble, I'll run."

Heat like she'd never felt before blasted through the open door along with smoke so dense that she could hardly breathe. Elijah nodded and slammed the door shut. She turned the corner and the setting sunrays lit up the hills giving the blazes life. They looked like graceful dancers vying for center stage as they danced across the hills, coming closer and closer to their ranch. She could see Gus and the guys herding scared cattle toward the house and barns, and could imagine cows bawling at calves and testy old bulls refusing to budge.

She squared up with the fence line, dropped the plow again, and started plowing. Smoke completely obliterated what was left of the sunset in her rear view. Hopefully, she and Elijah could keep it from jumping the fence and burning down their ranch.

She gunned the motor of the old tractor, promised it a week's rest if it didn't stop on her right there in the middle of the fire, and turned off the air conditioner. She could sweat, but she couldn't inhale smoke and keep driving. A fly buzzed around her head and she swatted at it.

"Suck in smoke and die. I don't have time to mess with you," she said.

It spiraled down to the seat beside her, wiggled a few times, and expired right there in the cab.

"I'll be danged! I didn't realize how powerful my words were. OK, Elijah, plow like the wind and meet me in front of the house." She giggled.

You are giddy. Slow down and hold the steering wheel tighter. You let that blasted fire ruin the ranch, and I'll haunt you forever. Aunt Maud's voice was back in her head.

"You already do," Sophie said aloud.

Before Aunt Maud could argue further, Sophie came out of the smoke, and the flames were so close to the tractor that they looked like they were coming right inside. They were so tall that she didn't think there was any way the firebreak would stop them, but miraculously the wind died down. The blaze stood still, not knowing where to go or what to do with no direction. It reminded Sophie of dancers with no music, milling about on the hardwood floor, wondering what to do next.

Then she heard the whirring noise of helicopter blades, and an enormous amount of water fell from the sky, some splashing on her tractor windows as it killed the flames right there, leaving charred posts and red-hot barbed wire where the huge bucket of water was dumped. The flames that didn't get squashed whipped up like a second-string football team during the last quarter of a shutout, tried to get enough momentum to jump the section line road when they hit it, but it was too much for them. The mission was over, and the ranch was still standing. No cattle were lost; not a single one with even a burn mark on it. The land lay like a green oasis in the middle of blackened fields with a few hot spots that continued to shoot up a single blaze every few minutes.

The fire had stomped its way across thousands of acres, but when the wind ceased, it didn't have the energy to jump the firebreak and continue its journey.

Elijah and Sophie parked their tractors at the same time and bailed out, each searching for the other one through the smoky distance. He waved when he saw her, and she held up a hand.

He covered the pasture in a few long, easy strides, thinking that the gray fog in front of him and her eyes were the same color. When he was only a few feet from her, their gazes locked and time stood still.

Nothing moved.

Not the smoke.

The last of the setting sun, barely an orange sliver at the end of blackened fields, didn't even sink lower.

"We did it," she said softly.

"Yes, we did," he said.

Gus yelled as he came toward them, breaking the moment. "We got them all inside pens. They ain't too happy, but I'd leave them right there until tomorrow. News said we might get rain. That'd settle the smell and the hot spots."

Elijah was disappointed. He'd wanted another few minutes alone with her. For a second, he'd wondered if the sparks from when their hands touched that afternoon had set the fire to burning in the first place. There'd sure been enough to blister his fingertips and make him want to draw her to his chest, maybe even see if those lips were as sweet as they looked.

"Sounds like they don't like their close quarters." Sophie giggled.

The sound of bawling cows was music to Elijah's ears, easing the tension from his tired arms and chest. He hadn't realized how uptight he'd been until that moment. He chuckled and it turned into laughter, which quickly changed to a full-fledged guffaw with Sophie laughing right along with him.

"It's not that funny," Gus said.

"No, it's not, but I'm so tickled that they're all alive that it made me giggle." Sophie wiped her eyes.

"You look like a coon with all that dirt and smoke on you," Elijah said.

"Well, you don't look any better," she said.

"Bawling cows are not funny!" Gus said.

Sophie patted him on the shoulder. "I know, Gus. It's just that laughter takes the bite out of the nerves. I was scared to death those flames were going to crawl right up in the tractor with me. I could feel the heat on the passenger's side of the tractor. When it all settles, I bet the paint is blistered bad. And then the wind died down, and the fire stopped right there at the fence. The barbed wire was red-hot, and the fence posts are black but still standing. I want you to put at least three men on the permanent payroll after the sale. We are going to redo the whole fence around the ranch with metal posts. If we'd been gone to another cattle sale or off to Walmart, this whole place would have been gone when we got back. We were lucky once but…"

"Woman, are you crazy? Metal posts won't stop a wildfire," Gus said.

"But they won't burn to the ground and leave us with cattle scattered from here to Hades," she said.

"You got that right. Y'all want a permanent job?" Gus turned around and asked the three men coming toward him.

"Bunkhouse rent is free. We can't offer medical insurance right now, but we'll pay time and a half for all over forty hours," Elijah said.

Frankie nodded. "Can I move in tomorrow? Rent is up on my apartment, and I was about to move back in with my folks."

"Yes, you can. You might have to clean it up, but there's room for six hands. Take your pick of the rooms," Elijah said.

"I'll take a job, but I want to be up-front and honest. If my old job comes up, I'll probably go back to it," Kendall said.

"Fair enough," Sophie said.

They both looked at Randy. He was the youngest of the three, graduating from high school the previous May. Short and stocky, he showed his Hispanic heritage in his dark hair, slightly toasted skin, and big brown eyes.

"I'm in if them two are. Six days a week. Off on Sunday?"

"Five and a half days a week. Off from noon on Saturday so y'all can do some two-steppin' with your girlfriends or some squirrel huntin'," Elijah said.

"Sounds good. I'll get my gear and be here tomorrow mornin'. Gus, you goin' to take us back to Baird or we goin' to stand around here and jaw all night?" Randy asked.

"Go get in the truck and remember that I'm your boss, so if I want to jaw until daylight comes rollin' in, I will, boy," Gus teased.

Randy air-punched him on the arm and then hopped into the back of the truck. "Whoooeee, boys! We got us jobs for the winter. I betcha you two can't keep up with me buildin' fence. I betcha I can string that barbed wire tighter and faster than either one of you."

"What are we bettin'?" Frankie, the best looking one of the crew asked. He had brown wavy hair and a face that reminded Sophie of a young Travis Tritt. She'd heard him play the guitar and sing when he worked in the hayfields in the summer and often wondered why the boy wasn't in Nashville.

Carolyn Brown

"Supper! Whoever does the most miles of fence a day don't have to cook in the bunkhouse," Randy said.

"I'll do the cookin'," Kendall told them. "I'd rather do it myself than take a chance on you two poisonin' me."

"We'll supply the beef, and you are welcome to whatever is left in the garden. There're peppers, cucumbers, and potatoes," Sophie said. "Freezer is full of beef from the last time we butchered around here. Help yourselves."

Kendall chuckled. "Now I'm sure I'll do the cookin'. Them two would burn up a good steak and make jerky out of a decent roast. We'll all be here tomorrow mornin', ma'am." He tipped his hat at her and hopped into the bed of the truck with Randy.

"You goin' to let any one of them ride up front?" Elijah asked Gus.

He shook his head. "Dirty as they are? No, I ain't. Besides, it'll teach them that I'm foreman and that has special rights."

Elijah was still laughing when Gus fired up the engine and drove away. He slung an arm around Sophie's shoulder, and together they walked toward the house, leaving the tractors parked.

"We really did it," he said again. "We faced down our first disaster and came through it. We're a good team, woman."

"Yes, we are," she said. "And I get the first shower."

"Hey, wait a minute."

She shrugged off his arm. "Ladies first."

"We are a team. We are not a couple," he protested.

"I don't care what you call it. You already had a shower."

He set his heels at the edge of the porch. "I'm twice as dirty and grimy now as when I got into the shower earlier. I shut off the air conditioner to keep the smoke out of the cab."

"So did I, and I'm having first shower," she said.

"You put up a fence. I'm putting in a second bathroom, and it's going to be right off my bedroom," he said.

"I like that idea, then you won't be cluttering up my bathroom." She opened the door and stepped inside the cool house.

He followed her and gasped when the cold air hit his sweaty skin. "Me, cluttering? It's not me who leaves makeup strewn on the counter and panty hose drying on the shower curtain."

She went straight for the bathroom. "Well I certainly hope that you don't leave makeup and panty hose in the bathroom." She giggled as she shut the door.

"Women!" He threw up his hands.

"What did you say?" she yelled through the door.

"I said that women are horrible creatures," he yelled back.

"We were made from a man's rib. That's pretty small, so if we are horrible when we…"

"Hush!" he yelled.

She swung the door open and walked right up to him. "Don't you ever tell me to hush. I'll talk when I want."

He leaned forward, cupped her cheeks in his hands, and kissed her soundly on the lips. She wrapped her arms around his neck and tangled her hands in his hair. When he pulled away, she took two steps back and reached up to see if her mouth was as warm as it felt. Surprisingly, her mouth was cool to the touch, but the tingles playing chase up and down her backbone were anything but cold.

She turned abruptly and went back into the bathroom, where she sat down on the edge of the tub for a long time before she was able to talk her weak knees into standing up.

It didn't help one bit that Elijah was whistling the Sammy Kershaw tune, "Don't Go Near the Water," that she'd been listening to earlier!

CHAPTER NINE

Sophie heard the bathroom door close behind Elijah when he went for his shower. She heard the water running, heard him singing "Hello Darlin'," an old Conway Twitty tune. So he liked country music. That didn't make him...she couldn't even think the words. She reached up and touched her lips again. They weren't warm, but they should have been from the way her heart kept skipping beats.

The cell phone on her bedside table rang, the tone telling her that it was either Kate or Fancy. She picked it up, not caring which one it was so long as they took her mind off Elijah.

"Did the fire come close to you? I saw it on the evening news. Looked like it was pretty close," Kate said.

"Close enough to blister the paint off the tractor I was plowing a firebreak with, and close enough that when the chopper dumped a bucket of water, it splashed all over my tractor," Sophie said.

"Mercy! Are y'all all right?"

"We saved all the cattle. Gus brought a crew and put the cattle in the pens and the front yard. They're bawling like crazy, but they're not burned. Tomorrow we'll turn the ones loose that we aren't selling. Kind of strange way of doing things, pen them up and then turn out what don't sell, rather than herding the ones for sale into the pens. I'm replacing fence posts starting the day after the sale. We've hired three guys who'll be in the bunkhouse full time, and at least if we have another fire, the posts will be metal and they won't burn to the ground. The old wood ones are just charred real bad, we didn't actually lose any of them and..."

"Sophie!" Kate raised her voice.

"What?"

"What really happened? You are talking too fast and furious for you. I know you, darlin'. You are the smart one of the three of us, and you keep your words close to home. Now what happened?"

"Elijah kissed me," Sophie blurted out.

"And?" Kate giggled.

"Don't laugh at me."

"I'm not! I'm just not surprised. You two are destined for each other."

Sophie gasped. "You're crazy, girl! You and Fancy both think because you found your three magic words that I'll find mine. Well, a single kiss doesn't make a life after wife situation."

"You are so right. How many does it take? Maybe you should go knock on his door and kiss him again to see if two kisses do the trick," Kate teased.

"Goodnight, Kate," Sophie said.

"I think the line was 'Goodnight, Irene'." Kate had started to giggle again.

"Then good-bye, Kate. See you in a couple of days." Sophie returned the phone back to her nightstand.

Elijah was singing Conway Twitty's "Tight Fittin' Jeans." He sang about a real lady, who normally wore pearls and high heels, going to a bar so she could be a good ole boy's girl. That he liked country music shocked Sophie. Riding a big Harley, wearing a do-rag with that little ponytail hanging down the back—it all pointed to hard rock, not old classic country.

She finally went to sleep but dreamed of blazes that reached from earth to heaven. She was on one side and Elijah was on the other. She could smell the smoke, feel the heat as it singed her hair, and hear him singing "Hello Darlin'." She wanted to strangle him until he turned blue, and then the big Harley came through the fire unscathed with Elijah riding it. He pointed to the passenger's seat behind him and extended a hand. She took it, hopped on, wrapped her hands around him, and in seconds they were riding beside a bubbling creek with bright green grass growing right up to the edge. The moon hung low in the sky, and stars twinkled around it like subjects bowing before a king.

Hard knocking on the door awoke her with a jerk. She threw a pillow over her head and groaned, but the rapping continued. She threw the pillow at the door and muttered. It went on. Fully awake, she looked at the clock and gasped. It was nine o'clock. The caterers would be there at ten, and her new crew was probably already in the bunkhouse.

She slung the door open to find Elijah standing there with a big grin on his handsome face.

"You going to sleep all day or do you want to help supervise the caterers?" he drawled.

"My alarm didn't go off," she said weakly.

Looking at him in those jeans, scuffed up boots, and T-shirt caused her breath to catch in her chest. Getting a whiff of Stetson aftershave sent her heart into double-time. Then she noticed that his ponytail was gone.

"What did you do to your hair?" she asked.

"Ran into Baird this morning and got a haircut. Figured it might look a little more respectable for a rancher," he said.

She was slightly disappointed. "You going to keep it cut all the time now?"

"No, ma'am. Probably get it cut once a year for the sale. Don't see much sense in all that expense and trouble through the year. Now, answer my question. You going to sleep, or are you getting up and having some breakfast with me?"

Sophie yawned. "I'm awake. You haven't eaten?"

"Nope. I told you I got a haircut. Stopped and got us some doughnuts for breakfast. Coffee is made. How long is it going to take you to get to the table?"

"Give me five minutes," she said.

He shut the door and she fell back on the bed. Life was certainly not boring with Elijah Jones in the house!

She gave herself one minute to think about how he'd looked without his ponytail, his black hair feathered back perfectly. Handsome didn't begin to describe him that morning, leaning on the doorjamb, a smile making his blue eyes twinkle. She could think of a dozen other words that did, and "sexy" topped out at number one.

She hopped up and grabbed a pair of jeans from the closet, then put them back on the hanger. It was going to be another hot day, so she chose a pair of denim shorts that barely reached her knee and a sleeveless chambray shirt that buttoned up the front. She swept her unruly curls up into a messy ponytail and put on a pair of socks before stomping her feet down into her oldest work boots.

The table was set with saucers, coffee cups, apple juice, and a dozen doughnuts stacked up pyramid-style in the middle of the table when she reached the kitchen. She pulled out a chair and sat down, picking a maple-frosted doughnut from the top of the stack.

Elijah grabbed a glazed doughnut at the same time, and their arms brushed against each other. Her bare arm barely touching his created a stirring down deep in his heart that he'd never experienced before. He'd dated women, lots of them, but not a one ever affected him like Sophie McSwain.

Sophie bit into the maple doughnut so she wouldn't have to say a word. The kiss wasn't a big Angus bull sitting at the table with them, creating awkwardness between them. But it had opened the floodgates for emotions that she thought she'd buried for good. Just his touch on her arm had sent tingles up and down her spine. Yes, sir, the quicker she could get this sale over with and go trailer shopping, the better.

"Barn looks really good. Guys have moved their gear into the bunkhouse, and they're out there giving it one more good sweeping before the caterers arrive this morning. We should be set up for finger foods and drinks when the first buyers come to look over the stock at noon," Elijah said.

Sophie knew all of that, except for the part about the three hired hands moving into the bunkhouse at the crack of dawn and sweeping out the barn, but she liked to listen to Elijah talk. His slow drawl sounded as if it was born in Texas or maybe Louisiana. She realized that she knew so little about him, and in the same instant, that she wanted to know everything.

"Where were you born and raised?"

Elijah chuckled. "Well, that sure came out of left field. I figured that you'd stomp your way to the kitchen fussin' about that kiss we shared and then give me what for about my plans all day."

"I might later," she said.

"OK, I was born in Silverton, Texas. It's out in the panhandle plains where there is nothing but dirt and sky. Go a few miles north and you'll fall off the world into the Tule and Palo Duro Canyons, but mostly it's flatland good for cattle and cotton. My folks had a big cotton operation, and I swore if I ever got away from cotton fields, I'd never go back. Dad died five years ago; Momma followed him the next year. My brothers and I sold the cotton farm and split the money. I wished a thousand times since then that I'd bought them out and kept it."

"If you had, would you have sold me your half of this place?"

"No."

"Why?"

He shrugged. "I like these rolling hills and trees, and I always felt peaceful when I visited Uncle Jesse and Aunt Maud here. When I found out I'd inherited half of the ranch, I felt like I was coming home."

"How many brothers do you have?"

"Eight."

She grabbed the juice and gulped it down to keep from choking.

"Eight! You are kiddin' me, right?"

"No. Momma wanted a girl so she kept trying to get one. All she got was nine boys. I'm right in the middle. Four older. Four younger."

"No girls?"

He shook his head. "You ought to go to one of our family reunions. Dad came from a big family. Had seven brothers and no sisters. There're only half a dozen cousins that are girls. The rest are guys. Makes a wonderful Sunday afternoon for football."

"I bet it does. What do those poor girls do?" Sophie asked.

"They play football with us. Joneses are tough," he grinned. "How about you? Got brothers?"

"I've got two sisters. Layla is just younger than I am, and Sandy is twenty-six. No brothers."

Elijah frowned. "Poor baby."

"What?" Sophie's hackles rose.

"A girl needs a big brother to protect her."

"And a boy needs at least one sister to learn about girls," she shot back.

He chuckled again. "Them two sisters redheaded spitfires like you?"

She shook her head. "No, they have brown hair and brown eyes like Momma. Daddy has black hair, but his grandmother was full-blood Irish, complete with red hair, green eyes, and a temper. I got the hair and temper from her, and the eyes from Daddy."

"Pretty nice combination, but you could have wallowed around in the temper DNA a little less," he said.

She bristled again. "And I suppose you don't have a temper?"

He grinned. "Of course I've got a temper, but my Indian blood keeps it in check."

"Yeah, right! On that note, I'm taking one more doughnut and heading to the barn. The caterer's wagons are pulling down the lane." She pointed to the kitchen window, and, sure enough, a line of trucks was pulling trailers going in that direction.

Elijah walked behind her, taking in the sight of her long legs. The shorts and cowboy boots were the finishing touch. She'd never been prettier than she was at that moment.

The barn was already crawling with people when they arrived. Kendall, Randy, and Frankie were helping carry folding tables of various sizes inside. The supervisor of the service was a big, burly man dressed in striped overalls, a chambray shirt with the sleeves rolled up, and dusty cowboy boots.

Sophie made introductions. "Hello, Tillman. Meet Elijah. He's half owner of the ranch now. We are running it together."

"He is not what I expected," Elijah said out of the corner of his mouth.

"Hush! You'll be amazed how well he cleans up when this part of the job is done," she whispered back.

Elijah took two more steps and stuck out his hand. "Good to meet you. Thank you for taking on extra days on such short notice."

Tillman's shake was bone crunching. "We didn't have nothing else on the calendar, so we're glad for the work. Ain't never seen this barn so clean. Looks like a dance hall instead of a sale barn. This is going to be a fun gig. Wish Maud would have given us a free hand like this."

"Sophie told you what we want?" Elijah asked.

"Yes, she did. We'll have it up and running by noon. Drinks ready for the lookers, and music playing," Tillman said.

Elijah looked at Sophie.

She shrugged. "No live band until the sale dance. Tillman has a nephew who's a DJ on a local radio station. He's brought some equipment, and he'll set up and keep country music going until ten tonight. Tomorrow, he'll start at eight in the morning and end at ten at night, and then the next day is the sale, so it'll be loud and noisy with the auctioneer."

"You take care of a lot," Elijah said.

Tillman nodded. "I'm a man of many talents."

"I believe it. What can I do to help?" Elijah asked.

"Well, you can take over my job supervisin' where the tables are to go and which way you want them lined up, and I'll go ahead and start a couple of grills back behind the barn and blow the smell inside. We'll be making shish kebabs with beef chunks for today's finger foods," Tillman threw over his shoulder as he headed toward the second trailer to tell the guys to unload the grills.

"So?" Sophie poked Elijah on the arm.

"All right! He's good, and I'm glad you hired him," Elijah said.

"Thank you. Did that hurt very much?"

"You punch like a girl. I've had mosquito bites that hurt worse," he said.

She giggled. "I wasn't talking about that little"—she stopped before she said "love tap" and paused—"that little air slap. I was talking about admitting that I was right to keep Tillman and his crew."

"Oh, honey, you will never know how bad that hurt." Elijah placed a hand over his heart and rolled his eyes. "But I won't die from the pain."

"Oh, stop the theatrics, and let's get on to our jobs. I was thinking that the tables should be set up randomly until the party night. Then we'll put them diagonally toward the dance floor so everyone can see the band."

Elijah nodded. "Sounds like a good plan to me. Give them room to talk and visit about the sale stock while they nibble on Tillman's finger foods. I was afraid you'd order cucumber sandwiches and fruit dip."

It was her turn to roll her eyes. "Aunt Maud would claw her way up out of that grave and use a peach tree switch on me for a stunt like that. This is a cattle sale. We'll serve beef in all its forms, from shish kebabs to steaks. Dang! Cucumber sandwiches? Give me a little credit."

Elijah threw back his head and roared. "Got you almost cussin' mad with just one sentence. You really did get your granny's temper."

At noon they both rushed back to the house to clean up for the first of the lookers. She took a fast shower and donned crisp, ironed designer jeans; her red cowboy boots; and a red-and-white-checked, Western-cut shirt with a wide lace yoke. She applied mousse to her curls, taming them into a manageable hairstyle, and slapped her new red cowboy hat on her head.

Elijah was waiting for her in the dining room. He wore creased jeans stacked up over black eel dress boots; a big silver buckle embossed with a bull rider; a white Western, pearl-snap shirt open at the neck; and he smelled like heaven on a stick.

Sophie clamped her jaw shut so tightly that it ached. But it kept it from falling open like a fish out of water.

Elijah offered her his arm. "You look pretty spiffy. One of these ranchers is liable to try to talk you into going home with him."

She slipped her arm through his. "Only one?"

"Maybe the one from Australia?"

"I scared him off last year. He doesn't want a woman who's got an Irish temper. He wants someone to walk two steps behind him and tell him how wonderful he is."

Elijah opened the door and stood to one side, but when they were outside, he tucked her arm back into his. It felt so right and natural, and maybe if the first of the prospective buyers saw them together, they wouldn't flirt with Sophie.

Yeah, right! his inner voice hollered at him. *They aren't blind, and she's a gorgeous woman. If you are interested, you'd best do more than offer her your arm.*

CHAPTER TEN

Sophie's face was frozen in a permanent smile. It's a wonder her head hadn't fallen completely off her shoulders from nodding at the buyers when they talked cattle and made cute ranching jokes. But she'd survived day one, and, even though it pained her to admit it, Elijah had been right. The buyers ate, drank, and stayed around longer than they did when refreshments weren't there.

Cowboys propped a leg up on the corral fence and studied the cattle, marking numbers in their books that Elijah provided right along with ink pens. Both had the ranch brand and logo on them, so they were a tax write-off.

At least he said they were when they arrived by mail the day before, and he'd assured her the overnight express postage and merchandise were a wise investment when her eyebrows had jacked up toward the ceiling. Aunt Maud would have thrown a Texas-size hissy at such nonsense, but Sophie noticed several buyers showing them off to one another.

Finally, the day ended. The new ranch hands were tucked away in the bunkhouse. Frankie said they weren't making food out there that night because they'd all sampled Tillman's kebabs all day. Sophie had been too nervous for anything more than a taste of the meat, peppers, and onions, so after her shower that evening, she was starving. She padded to the kitchen in her cotton terry-cloth robe and opened the refrigerator.

"Ain't much there. I'm havin' bologna and cheese," Elijah whispered.

His warm breath on her still wet neck sent tingles down her spine. She straightened up so fast she bumped her shoulder on the refrigerator door.

"Why are you eating in the dark?" she asked.

"Don't need a light to chew and swallow," he said.

She left the refrigerator door hanging and flipped the light switch. When she turned around, Elijah was barely a foot from her. He wore plaid cotton pajama bottoms and a gauze undershirt that stretched over his muscles. The bologna and cheese sandwich in his hands was half gone, and a Dr Pepper sat on the cabinet beside him.

"You're all out of Pepsi," he said hoarsely. He'd thought she was gorgeous in her cowgirl getup that afternoon, but she was something else with her white fluffy robe belted around her tiny waist, a towel wrapped turban-style around her head, and bare feet.

She pulled out bologna, cheese, mustard, pickles, lettuce, tomatoes, and one of his Dr Peppers. He wanted to argue, but he couldn't find enough air in his deflated lungs to say a word.

Sophie ignored him and went about making a sandwich. She'd buy him a whole case of soda pop to replace the one she intended to drink right then, but she was not going to put it back if she had to whip his sorry rear end with one hand tied behind her. She'd hang onto her sandwich in her whipping hand and bet dollars to cow chips that she didn't even squash it during the fight. She was that thirsty, and iced tea just didn't sound good.

"That looks pretty good," he said.

"Want one?"

He nodded.

"It's my famous sandwich. Worth a lot," she told him.

"I won't gripe about the Dr Pepper, if you'll make me one." He watched her slice the tomatoes thin and place them between the cheese and meat.

"Deal!" she said.

He chuckled. "I was too busy all day long to eat much, but it smelled good, didn't it?"

"Oh, yeah! It was a wonderful idea. Kept the folks here, and the notepads and pens were a nice touch, too," she said.

Elijah's jaw went slack, and his mouth fell open. He was almighty glad there was no food in it. He popped his palm against the side of his head as if trying to knock something out of his ear.

"Oh, stop it." Sophie laughed. "I'm not a coldhearted witch. I admit it when something is a good idea and works. Here, you can have this one, and I'll make another for myself." She cut it in half diagonally and handed the plate to him. "Throw a few barbecue potato chips on the side and you've got a meal fit for the gods."

He opened the cabinet, rustled around until he found the chips, and carried them to the table. "Where'd you learn to make this?"

"At home. My dead ex-husband hated sandwiches. I can cook, but he made enough money that he hired a maid and a cook. She made meals to his specifications. Sometimes I got so tired of fancy food that I picked at it and later snuck off to the kitchen for a bologna and cheese sandwich. I've eaten dozens of them sitting on the floor with the refrigerator door open for light."

"Was he crazy? You should have sent him over to the war zone. Let him live on dehydrated soup and canned meat for a year, and he'd think he'd died and gone to heaven to get bologna and cheese," Elijah said between bites.

"He was raised in a wealthy household and used to that kind of thing. I was raised up in a middle-class house. Oil and water don't mix," she said.

"What really happened between y'all?"

"He married me because he wanted a wife. Single television evangelists do not do as well as married ones. But he also wanted to continue to chase skirts. I have to admit that he was very discreet. I had no idea until I found a note and a jewelry receipt one day. A little investigation on my part, and a bunch of investigation on the part of a P.I., turned up more than I wanted to know. I was going to confront him about it, but he died in a plane crash on the way home. There were two women in the plane with him. His father and the publicist paid their families off and wanted to give me money to keep quiet," she said.

Not once had Sophie been to a therapist. Aunt Maud had had to drag the story out of her, and right there in the kitchen she'd told Elijah the whole thing without batting an eye. She'd actually told him more than she'd even told Kate and Fancy. What in the devil had gotten into her?

"Did you take the money?" Elijah asked.

She shook her head and the towel fell off. Her hair hung in tight little ringlets, water droplets hanging inside the curls like dew drops on red roses. "There was this enormous insurance policy that quadrupled if he was killed on an airplane. I didn't want or need their hush money. Aunt Maud rescued me and brought me here. It's home, Elijah, and I meant it when I said I'd buy your half." She sat down at the table and reached into the chip bag.

He laid a hand on her arm. "I know you did. And I was serious about buying you out. We had a big farm out in West Texas. Even split nine ways, I've got the money to do it; plus, I lived simply for the past twenty years, so there's my military savings. But I've got to be honest, Sophie. I like having a partner. Uncle Jesse used to say that a ranch needs a woman. I expect it does, but it doesn't have to be a wife, does it?"

His touch on her arm felt as if he was branding it with hot steam. She was sure there would be a hand-shaped burn print when he removed it, but there wasn't. So he wasn't interested in anything permanent other than friendship. She could do that…as long as he kept his kisses to himself.

They hit the ground running the next morning. The smell of smoked ribs filled the air when they walked out the back door together: Sophie in her mint-green T-shirt with the rhinestone outline of a longhorn bull on the back, her green cowboy boots, and a fresh pair of starched jeans. Elijah wore a white shirt, starched jeans, and his boots had been polished to a shine.

They were dragged off into two different directions the moment the early-bird buyers spotted Elijah and Tillman saw Sophie. She was soon knee-deep supervising the waiting staff and being nice to everyone. Her smile was more genuine that day and didn't hurt her cheeks nearly so badly.

"I'm doing ribs, brisket, and we've got coleslaw and potato salad to put out on the table. Until lunchtime, I've got cold roast beef and barbecued pulled pork on the tables for the early birds to make sandwiches. Did I forget anything?" Tillman asked.

"Sounds like you've got it under control. Keep the soda pop iced down in the tubs and the sweet tea and lemonade pitchers full, and we'll be all right. It's going to be another scorcher, and they'll be thirsty all the time," Sophie answered.

"From the looks of the crowd, I'd say we're going to have a bumper-crop sale this year. Your aunt Maud would have fought you on the extra expense, but it's going to bring in a heck of a profit," Tillman said.

Sophie nodded. "You are right. I've never seen so many buyers."

"Y'all was lucky that the fire didn't shut you down."

Sophie wiped the back of her hand across her forehead. "I was scared stiff for a while there. I thought for sure we were going up in blazes, but the firebreak plus those big buckets of water the helicopters dropped put an end to it. Still, it burned right up to three sides of us."

"Hard work and luck," Tillman said.

"Hey, girl," Kate yelled and waved from across the yard.

Hart had let her out, and he was driving the trailer on out to the pens where he'd unload his stock for the sale. Several men were already walking in that direction to see what new cattle were arriving.

"Mercy, but that smells wonderful. When's it going to be ready?" Kate asked.

"Noon. But if you are hungry there's food in the barn." Sophie looped her arm in Kate's.

"I'm always hungry."

Sophie pulled her toward the big open doors. "And hunger always makes you cranky. So come on and we'll find something to eat. I didn't have time for breakfast."

"So did he kiss you again?" Kate whispered as they walked away from Tillman.

Sophie blushed crimson. "No! But I think we might be friends. He's not interested in marriage, Kate. It's not like it was with you and Hart. Y'all had so much heat between you that a person sunburned just standing close to you. With me and Elijah, it's barely tolerance. But it could develop into friendship in time. I'm tired of fighting him for the ranch already, so I'm going to buy a trailer and put it on the backside, over by the other section line road, so I can come and go as I please. I've already got a spot picked out."

"Make him get the trailer or build a house. You were here first," Kate said.

"Actually, I want to be the one to move out. I think it'll be good for me. I went from my parents' house to a dorm room and then into marriage. I've never had my very own place like you did in Louisiana and Fancy did down in Florida," Sophie said.

Kate stopped in front of the long table and sighed. "This all looks so good, I don't know where to start. When we have our next sale, I'm going to make Hart do it like this. You'll tell me how much percentage it ups the profits?"

Sophie handed her a plate. "Sure I will. And much as I hate to give a point to Elijah, it was his idea. We've had more buyers out here looking around than we ever did before. And

I think it's because of the food and drinks. Oh, and maybe the notepads and pens."

"What?" Kate filled her plate to overflowing with two big sandwiches and barbecue chips.

"Elijah got this bright idea to order ballpoint pens and notepads with the ranch logo on them so the buyers could make notes about what cattle they were interested in buying," she explained.

"The man is a genius. If you don't kiss him again, you are an idiot, and I don't have to be the borderline fool anymore." Kate headed to a table, her long black hair swinging down her back. She'd dressed in shorts, cowboy boots, and a Western-cut shirt, and she looked every bit the part of a rancher's wife. No one would ever guess that she had a degree in criminal justice and had been a fantastic detective down in New Iberia, Louisiana.

Sophie finished preparing a pulled pork sandwich and carried it to the table. Kate was making noises that said the food was good and nodding her head at Sophie. "How long in advance do I have to book Tillman?" she asked between bites.

"I have no idea. He was able to bring his crew out here for the whole three days on a day's notice, but we've had him down to work the sale party for a year. You might want to talk to him if you really want him to do your sale next spring. I'm tellin' you, he's good. Yesterday he made shish kebabs and called it finger food," Sophie answered.

"What's on for supper?" Kate asked.

"Same thing. Ribs and brisket from noon until they shut it down at ten tonight. Then tomorrow he's setting up for dinner with hamburgers during the sale. After that his crew, plus our three new hired hands, are going to power wash the floors and set up tables for the party tomorrow night. He's making all of the regular barbecue-type foods for supper plus grilled shrimp, T-bone steaks, and some fancy kinds of desserts," Sophie said.

"Wow! I'm getting my name on the calendar soon as I get finished. But first, tell me about this Elijah friendship thing," Kate said.

"He's easy to talk to," Sophie said.

"Something that pretty would be."

"You think he's good-lookin'?"

"Are you stone-cold blind, woman?" Kate gasped.

Maybe I am. Maybe I've had too much pain in my heart and it's made me blind, Sophie thought.

"Is Fancy coming with Theron?" She changed the subject.

"No, she doesn't want to get the baby or Tina out in this heat. But she'll be at the party tomorrow night. I made her promise to keep her housekeeper and babysitter there all night and get out. She hasn't left the baby yet, so it's going to be a tough time for her. We'll have to rally round and convince her that it's OK," Kate said.

Sophie nodded, but her thoughts stayed on Kate's comment about her being blind. Was Elijah trying to tell her that he was interested when he kissed her, or had it just been a fluke thing? Something that happened in the moment and then he regretted it, so that's why he said that about a ranch needing a woman but not necessarily a wife.

"Well, it don't need a man. Me and Aunt Maud proved that," she mumbled.

"What?" Kate asked.

Sophie explained what Elijah had said and where her thoughts had been. After all, there was precious little in her life that Kate didn't already know, and what she didn't, she'd bug the dickens out of Sophie until she got it.

Kate listened, alternately shaking her head and nodding. "Way I see it is that you two got a lot of baggage between you to get rid of. You don't have to hurry. You got time."

"Well, thank you for that. Does it mean I don't have to go out on dates every Friday and Saturday night?" Sophie asked.

"Oh, no, it don't mean that at all. Either you go out with Elijah, or we're going to fix you up. It's time you crawled out of that black hole you been livin' in and get out into the world again," Kate said.

The day ended just like it began: in a whirlwind of preparation for the sale the next day. It was midnight when Sophie finally crawled into bed. She figured she'd be asleep when her head hit the pillow, but one of the songs she heard played that day kept running through her mind like it was on a continuous loop. Lee Ann Womack singing "I Hope You Dance."

She hummed the song but couldn't remember all the lyrics, and it was driving her stark-raving mad. Finally she turned on the light, picked up her iPod, and found the song.

A dam let loose in her soul, and she wept as she listened to Lee Ann sing words that cut the chains from her heart. The lyrics said that she hoped love would never leave the listener empty-handed. When she said that whenever one door closed she hoped another opened, and asked the listener to promise to give faith a fighting chance, Sophie put her hands over her eyes and sobbed.

Lee Ann sang about never fearing the mountains in the distance and never settling for the path of least resistance. She mentioned that living meant taking chances, and loving might be a big mistake but it was worth making.

"Is it?" Sophie pulled two tissues from the box on the nightstand and blew her nose.

She hummed along with tears still streaming down her face as Lee Ann ended the song by saying that when someone got the chance to sit it out or dance, she hoped she danced.

Sophie wept through a dozen more tissues and fell asleep with a burden lifted from her soul. It was the first time she'd cried since the day the policeman came to her door with the news that her cheating husband had died in a plane crash.

CHAPTER ELEVEN

The rude alarm clock awoke Sophie at six o'clock from a dream she didn't want to leave. It was aggravating when she sat up and opened her eyes that she could only remember it was about Elijah. No matter how hard she tried, she couldn't remember what they were doing or where they were in the dream.

Rattling pots and pans in the kitchen said he was already up. It was Saturday and…

"Sale day!" She squeaked and jumped out of bed, forgetting about dreams, tears, and Lee Ann Womack's song. Sale day was the single most important day on a ranch, and the sale this year was doubly important. The buyers would see a solid, unified front between the partnership and that the ranch had survived the fire.

She belted a red silk kimono robe round her middle and padded to the kitchen where Elijah was making pancakes and sausage. He turned when he felt her presence behind him and felt another tug on his heart. Sophie, all sleepy and wearing a bright red robe, was just as beautiful as Sophie in her jeans and boots. Elijah didn't want to fall for Sophie. He wanted to buy her half of the ranch, run it with the help of a few hired hands, and enjoy the peace and quiet of ranching. That great big *M word* did not have a place in his plans.

"Good morning. Ready to see how we've done in our short time on the ranch?"

She cut her eyes up at him. "You're the short-time partner, Elijah Jones. I've been here almost two years, buddy."

"Grouchy this morning, are we?"

She air-slapped his arm. "No, I'm not cranky, and you aren't going to rile me up. This is sale day. Something I've worked toward for a year, and I want to show Aunt Maud that she taught me well."

He flipped two pancakes onto a plate, added a couple of sausage patties, and handed it to her. "She knows you are capable. Even if the sale is a complete bust, believe me, Aunt Maud knows."

"Thank you. For the breakfast, that is. And how do you know that about her?" Sophie carried the plate to the table, sat down, and slathered the hot pancakes with pats of butter.

"She wrote me a letter once a week, faithfully. It was always dated Sunday afternoon and postmarked Monday. And after you moved to the ranch, she talked a lot about you and how you were 'catchin' right on,' as she put it," Elijah said.

Sophie swallowed the lump in her throat. So while Sophie was in Albany with her friends, Aunt Maud spent her Sundays writing letters to Elijah and saying nice things about her.

"What else did she write to you about?" she asked.

"Honey, Aunt Maud kept me so well-informed about every cow on the place, and how much hay this pasture produced or wheat that one did, that I could run this place in my sleep. I kept notes in a book because she told me to, and I'm glad I did, because now I'm not running around in the dark. She even made suggestions about which cattle needed to go to the sale today and told me to invite Theron and Hart to bring their fall culls to our sale, but not to let in anyone else. She said that Theron and Hart let her bring to their spring sales so it was a trade-off, but if we started letting every freeloader in the county into our sale, pretty soon we'd be footin' the bill for everyone."

Sophie managed a weak giggle. "That sounds just like her."

Elijah joined her at the table with a huge stack of steaming hot pancakes and a whole plate of sausage patties that he set between them. "Two little old sausages ain't goin' to hold you through the whole sale. Eat up, girl, we got quite a mornin' ahead of us."

She forked two more patties to her plate, covered the pancakes with warmed maple syrup, and cut off a bite. "Mmmm, good! You share recipes?"

"No, you want those pancakes, you got to ask me to make them," he said.

"Meanie!"

He grinned. "Yep, that I am."

"OK, then while we eat tell me about your brothers. You didn't even tell me their names," she said. "Besides, you've been getting letters about me ever since I moved here, and I don't know hardly anything about you."

Elijah swallowed and sipped hot black coffee. "Matthew, Mark, Luke, and John."

"I didn't ask you to recite the books of the Bible," she said.

"I'm not. Those're my four older brothers. Matthew is fifty-two, Mark is fifty, Luke is forty-eight, and John is forty-six. Momma gave up on havin' a girl when John was born. She was twenty when Matthew was born, and the old folks out in West Texas say it's not good to have kids when you are past thirty. I kind of snuck up on her and Dad when she was thirty-two. Then they got Jed when I was two and Noah when I was four. By then she said she could live without a daughter and seven boys were enough kids. The older four were all teenagers, and I was eight when she got pregnant at the age of forty. I remember it well, because she was sure she was going to have a sweet little daughter. She got twin boys: Tanner and Hayden, who were thirty-two this past summer."

"Tanner and Hayden? All the rest of you have Bible names," Sophie said.

"Guess she gave up on God blessin' her with a girl when she had two more mean old boys at forty. Matthew got married the year before the twins were born, and Momma got her first granddaughter just a few weeks after she gave birth to the twins. That granddaughter is married now and has three kids of her own. It's a big family reunion, but like I told you before, there ain't many girls at it."

Sophie finished off the last of her breakfast and poured herself a cup of coffee. "Sounds like it. And the twins, are they married, too?"

"No, just me and the youngest two are still runnin' from the noose. Oh, I forgot to tell you, Tanner and Hayden are coming to the sale. They're between jobs, and they've got lots of experience on a ranch. Tanner's been foreman of a big operation for the past five years. Owner sold it last week. Hayden taught agriculture at the high school in Silverton, but he's not renewing his contract. Says he's had all he can stand of teaching, and he'd rather ranch. I'd like for us to have a sit-down visit, the four of us, after the sale is finished. I've got some ideas," Elijah said.

Sophie rolled her eyes and carried her plate to the dishwasher. Elijah always had "ideas" and she was running as fast as she could to stay up with him already. Now what did he have up his sleeve?

❖ ❖ ❖

At ten o'clock the barn was full, the balconies elbow to elbow, the sale floor crowded, and caterers were weaving in among the people with trays of ice-cold soda pop and sweet tea. The refreshment table offered little yeast rolls stuffed with barbecued beef, ham, a delicious cream cheese with a faint pineapple flavor, and pulled pork, as well as three-tiered trays with petit fours and bite-size pieces of cheesecake in a dozen flavors.

At noon Tillman would bring out the ribs and brisket. At three the sale would be over, and they'd have to hustle to get the barn ready for the big party, which started at seven with buffet supper and a live band.

When the auctioneer took his place and the first heifer was brought into the circular sale pen, butterflies began doing a fast line dance in Sophie's stomach. She and Elijah were sitting on the top bleacher in the south-side balcony. She held a copy of the sale book in her lap; both she and Elijah wore worried expressions. That cow down there would set the precedent for the whole sale. If she went at above fair market price because of her excellent bloodlines, then the rest of the sale had a pretty good chance at doing the same. If she sold for next to nothing, they'd be running in the red next year.

Even if they had a lean year, Sophie had enough money in her personal bank account that she did not intend to go to the bank for a loan. Aunt Maud had never borrowed against the land, and Sophie wasn't starting now, no matter what this great plan of Elijah's was.

The smell of so many bodies (so much perfume from the ladies and aftershave from the gents), blended with the odor of cows, blowing dust, and the faint scent of burned land added to the excitement of the first sale of the day. Conversational chatter slowly died when the microphone emitted a high-pitched squeak as the auctioneer adjusted it.

Sophie wasn't sure when she and Elijah laced their fingers together until he squeezed her hand. She looked up and their eyes locked, neither of them saying a word, yet reading each other's thoughts as clearly as if they were written in indelible ink on their faces.

"It's OK," he finally said. "Breathe."

"I can't until this first cow is sold. Aunt Maud always laughed at me but…"

Elijah leaned down and whispered. "Stop worryin'. It's taken care of."

She turned her head at a slant and looked at him. "What?"

"I know what every cow is worth. They are not selling beneath their value."

"And you can control that how? Are you magic?"

He shook his head. "No, I have a personal buyer on the floor. Couple of them. Tanner and Hayden. They have a note-book, and if that cow doesn't sell for what's in the book, they'll bid on her."

"Is that legal? You are buying your own cattle." Sophie frowned.

"Yes, it's legal. Actually, they're buying the cattle with my money. I told you I have a plan," he said.

"That scares me worse than anything."

The auctioneer made the black cow in the pen sound like her hooves were studded with diamonds and then began his lightning-fast sales pitch. When the final bid was in, Sophie could hardly believe the number that she wrote into her book. It was going to be a fantastic sale if it kept going like that.

"My brothers did not have to raise their cards. That one is going over to Breckenridge to Hart's neighbor." Elijah's voice held as much excitement as Sophie's heart did.

The cows were all sold by noon, and neither Tanner nor Hayden had bought a single one. In between cattle coming into the auction pen and those that had sold leaving it, Sophie had tried to figure out which of the cowboys were Elijah's brothers, but the crowd was too dense. The auctioneer announced that there would be an hour break for everyone to have lunch and then the bull sale would start at one o'clock.

Sophie let out a whoosh of air. "We've done good so far."

"Yes, we have." Elijah squeezed her hand one more time then let it go. "Let's go mingle among the buyers and have some lunch."

"Where are your brothers?" she asked.

"Right here." a deep voice said from right behind her. "I'm Tanner, the good-lookin' twin, and this is Hayden, the smart one."

She turned to find two cowboys standing against the wall. They weren't quite as tall as Elijah, but they had the same jet-black hair. Their eyes were brown, and if it hadn't been for different-colored shirts, she couldn't have told them apart. Tanner wore a yellow knit shirt, and Hayden had on a pearl-snap blue plaid.

"Don't let him kid you. I got the good looks *and* the brains. All he got was good looks," Hayden teased. "Elijah didn't tell us that you were beautiful as well as smart. Guess me and you got a lot in common."

Elijah actually blushed. "Don't be usin' that flirtin' line on Sophie. She's way too smart to fall for the likes of you."

He realized in that moment that his two brothers were a whole lot closer to Sophie's age than he was, and a wicked lightning bolt of pure jealousy shot through his heart.

Hayden grinned and punched his older brother on the arm. "My flirtin' lines are just fine, brother, and you'd do well to take some lessons from me. Forty years old and still not a filly roped in. I'd stay away from him if I was you, Miz Sophie."

Elijah stood up and offered a hand to Sophie, who took it, but he didn't let go when she was on her feet. "Come on, you two old renegades. If Sophie doesn't mind, we'll sit with you at dinner. Looks like the line is already formin' at the buffet table, but Tillman says he can put three hundred or more through in less than twenty minutes. I swear the man works magic."

Sophie suddenly found herself surrounded by tall, dark cowboys as they made their way down the stairs toward the food tables. And she was hungry. The butterflies had flown away after the first couple of cows had sold so well, and her pancake breakfast was long gone.

"Hey, lookin' good." Kate winked.

"I'm pleased with what my cows brought. Hope my two bulls do as well," Hart said.

"Meet my brothers, Tanner and Hayden. This is Hart and Kate Ducaine, friends and fellow ranchers from over near Breckenridge." Elijah dropped Sophie's hand and made introductions.

Kate raised an eyebrow at Sophie and she shrugged. Hand-holding did not mean saying vows in front of a preacher.

"Y'all come on and sit with us," Elijah said.

"Glad to. So what did you two think of the sale?" Hart asked the twins.

Sophie tuned them out and refused to look at Kate again. She loaded her plate with brisket, added a bowl of pinto beans and a chunk of cornbread, and headed toward the nearest table with room for six people. She set her plate down and started to pull out a chair only to have Hayden do it for her and sit beside her on the right. Elijah claimed the chair on her left, and Hart, Kate, and Tanner sat across the table.

An old friend of Maud's, Myrle, claimed the end of the table. She wore her dyed red hair ratted up into a tall hairdo that went out of style in the sixties. Her jeans were skin-tight, and her Western shirt was tucked in behind a belt with a rhinestone double-heart buckle. "Sale is going good. I bought a cow with a calf beside her to beef up my stock a little. Was glad to get it, too. I thought that old man beside me was going to take her home, and I made up my mind if he couldn't even flirt with me, he darn sure wasn't getting that cow."

"What idiot wouldn't flirt with a gorgeous lady like you?" Hayden asked. "By the way, darlin', I'm Hayden Jones. Elijah is my older brother—much, much older—and this other kid over here is my twin brother, Tanner. He's kinda shy, but I know that he's admirin' you from afar."

Myrle giggled. "You are full of cow chips, darlin', but even a sixty-year-old woman likes a little flirtin'. You, darlin', might have gotten that cow at a good price if you'd been sittin' beside me."

Kate cleared her throat.

"OK, smarty-pants, so I'm a few years on the other side of sixty. Don't tell these precious cowboys. Let me have my ego boost for the day," Myrle said.

Kate nodded. "Just so long as you admit you are sixty-one."

Myrle winked. "Yes ma'am."

They both knew that Myrle had passed her eightieth birthday more than a year ago, and that she still liked to chase after any man who could square dance or even two-step her around the dance floor. She had a ranch outside of Albany and ran it with a firm hand and an eye for good cattle.

"I'm lookin' for a good Angus bull today. Hart, did you bring that big old bruiser that I been buggin' you about?" Myrle asked.

"No, ma'am. That bull ain't never goin' to be for sale. He's producin' a calf crop that is sellin' high every spring," Hart said.

"Well, dang it! What you got...hey, Theron, come on over. We got room for one more. You got any bulls for sale?"

Theron carried his plate to the end of the table and settled in before he answered. "No, Miz Myrle. I brought a few heifers, couple with calves beside them, but no bulls. I'm savin' them for the spring sale at my place. I did well this mornin', Elijah. Thank you for inviting me to add to your sale."

"And Sophie?" Kate shot Theron a dirty look.

"Sorry about that. Didn't mean to slight you, Sophie. Y'all have both done up your sale right well. I've already talked to Tillman and booked him for ours next spring. You should be out among the buyers. They're all talkin' about how this is the best sale they've seen in years. The food has been good, and the fact they don't have to go into town for every meal is great."

"Next year, I'm thinkin' of putting in some trailer spaces for the ones who want to park here," Sophie said.

Elijah jerked his head around to stare at her.

"Don't be thinkin' you're the only one with big plans in the makin'," Sophie told him.

Kate burst out in a guffaw that had people looking to see what was so funny at the owner's table. Tanner and Hayden joined in first and then the rest of the table.

"Looks to me like my big brother done met his match," Hayden said when the laughter died down.

Kate wiped her eyes with the big, square red bandanna that Tillman provided in lieu of napkins. "Looks to me like my friend met hers, too."

CHAPTER TWELVE

Sophie dressed in a long, denim prairie skirt; an ecru-colored satin camisole covered by a light beige, lace, Western-cut blouse with tiny pearl buttons up the front and from wrist to elbow on the sleeves; and new, tan cowgirl boots. She swept her hair up into a messy French roll, letting the curls fall where they wanted. Then she added a chunky, silver heart-shaped necklace and matching dangling earrings.

"Ready or not, here I come," she whispered to her reflection in the mirror.

The bull sale that afternoon had been even more spectacular than the morning sale. Aunt Maud was probably kicking up the angel dust on the streets of heaven as she danced around. She was smiling at that idea when she headed for the living room.

She thought of Johnny Cash when she saw Elijah in his matching black Western shirt, slacks, and polished eel boots. His silver belt buckle had even been shined up and his hair slicked back. His brothers both wore starched jeans, white shirts open at the neck, and boots. Their belt buckles were also silver, but they didn't shine like Elijah's.

"Whoo-wee," Hayden whistled through his teeth. "You'll be the prettiest girl at the party tonight, Miz Sophie. You will save this humble old cowboy one dance, won't you?"

Sophie couldn't help but smile. "Hayden, there's not a humble bone in your body."

"Joneses had a choice when we was born. We could be humble or good-lookin'. Most of us chose good-lookin'. Elijah, now he's the exception. He chose neither one and decided he'd be a hero instead," Tanner said. His voice was deeper than Hayden's and his drawl more pronounced.

"Is that right? Well, while we are dancin' tonight, you two will have to tell me all about his heroism," Sophie said.

"And while we are dancin', I'll tell you not to believe anything they say," Elijah said.

"Wait a minute. Who says she can dance with you?" Hayden teased.

"Who's big enough to say she can't?" Elijah asked.

Sophie felt like a queen among a bunch of knights. Maybe not in shining armor, more like in shining Western gear. She enjoyed the easy banter and the camaraderie between the brothers. She'd never had that with her sisters. Maybe it was because Elijah was eight years older than the twins, and she and her two sisters were so close in age.

"We don't have time to jaw with you two. We have to be at the doors when the party starts. So y'all can stay in here and make a grand entrance or you can come with us. Take your choice." Elijah offered his arm to Sophie.

She looped hers inside it and wasn't even shocked at the little sparks that danced around them. She'd admit that she was attracted to Elijah Jones. A woman would have to be stone-cold blind not to be. If she could see him all decked out in black, wearing that wonderful aftershave, or if she could hear his deep southern drawl when he talked, she'd be attracted to him. It did not mean that anything would come of it.

"We're going to hang back for half an hour and watch some television. We want to make the entrance," Tanner said.

"Suit yourselves," Elijah threw over his shoulder as he and Sophie left the house.

There wasn't even a hint of a breeze, and the thermometer still shot up close to the three-digit number. Sophie was glad that Tillman had brought in the big air conditioner units and the barn was cool.

After the sale was finished that afternoon and everyone cleared out, Gus had commanded a team that quickly removed the pen from the center of the barn and then brought in the power washer to clean up the floor. In three hours, the barn was transformed from a sale barn to a party barn with bales of hay set up to separate the dance floor from the band and tables lined up diagonally and covered with crisp white cloths. Tillman even brought bolts of red, white, and blue illusion and draped the walls from balcony rails to floor. When he turned on his portable air conditioners, the thin illusion flowed like a gentle breeze was chasing through the barn. Red carnations in milk-white, glass bud vases decorated the tables, along with candles set in wrought iron holders made from horseshoes and covered with glass globes to keep the wind from blowing out the flames.

"Wow!" Sophie exclaimed when they stepped inside the barn doors.

"Looks great, don't it? Just what I imagined for this year's sale. Next year we'll do something different," Elijah said.

"Such as?"

"Different theme mainly for the party. The rest I'd like to keep pretty much the same. We'll get a reputation for having a fantastic sale, and it'll keep the buyers coming back. Did you know that Aussie bought two bulls and he's having them shipped all the way over there? He invited us to come to his sale in October. Want to go to Australia?"

Sophie was stunned. "Are you serious?"

Hart and Kate entered the barn before Elijah could answer.

"Don't you two look happy," Kate said.

"We are happy. We had a fabulous sale today. Glad y'all came back for the party. You are the first ones here so help yourself to the food," Elijah said.

"That's not fair to the other guests." Hart's eyes twinkled. "Kate can eat a whole steer when she's hungry. Once she gets full, there might not be anything left."

Kate slapped his arm. She'd chosen a red satin shirt that night, sleeveless with rhinestone buttons and trim on the yoke; red boots; and a bright red flower in her black hair to set it off.

Sophie hugged her. "You are beautiful."

"No, Fancy is the pretty one. You are the smart one, and you know what that makes me, but thank you." Kate laughed and dragged Hart toward the food tables where waiters in white shirts and black slacks waited to help them with whatever they wanted.

"What was that all about?" Elijah asked.

"Ever hear that old song by K.T. Oslin called '80's Ladies'?"

He nodded.

"Well, there's a line in it that says one was pretty, one was smart, and one was a borderline fool. When we all got together last year at Fancy's grandma's house and figured out that we were all living back in this area, we were talking and Kate said that Fancy was the pretty one, I was the smart one, and she was the borderline fool."

"Why?"

"Fancy's always been petite and cute," Sophie said.

"And you are smart, no doubt about that," Elijah said.

Her heart floated above her body for a few minutes at that compliment.

"Why was Kate the borderline fool?" he asked.

"Because she couldn't get Hart Ducaine out of her heart. She fell in love with him when she was fifteen and measured every other man by his yardstick," Sophie said.

"I see," Elijah said.

"Fancy!" Sophie squealed. "You came."

Fancy and Theron looked so darn cute together. It was like fate put them in Albany, Texas, at the same time just so they'd meet. Fancy at four feet eleven inches and Theron at barely five feet two were perfect for each other. Fancy had chosen a long skirt much like Sophie's for the party but topped hers off with a bright yellow shirt that set off her blonde hair and big blue eyes.

"Of course, I wouldn't miss your sale for anything," Fancy said.

"And besides, my mother and dad came for the weekend so she's not worried about Glory," Theron said.

"I thought we were calling her Emma-Gwen," Sophie said.

"We did too, but Tina says she looks like a Glory and it's stuck," Fancy said. "Come on, darlin', I see food."

Theron shook hands with Elijah and said, "She's only called home four times since we left Albany."

"Oh, don't be tellin' on me now." Fancy tugged at his hand.

Theron winked at Sophie and allowed Fancy to drag him off to the food table and then over to where Kate and Hart were seated.

The guests came in spurts. Half a dozen, then twenty, and then a whole trainload. At eight o'clock Hayden and Tanner made their appearance, ate, and were dancing by eight thirty.

"My feet hurt. My face is about to freeze forever in this expression. And I really need something to drink," Sophie said.

"I suppose we've done our duty. Let's get a beer and mingle. Hungry?" Elijah asked.

"Starving. Let's eat first and then mingle," she suggested.

He put his hand on the small of her back and guided her toward the table. From past experience she knew that there wouldn't be a red mark on her back where he touched her, but it sure felt extra warm. They fixed plates and carried them to the table where their friends had saved two chairs.

The dance floor was full, the band playing one country song after another, from Conway Twitty to the Zac Brown Band and everything in between. Fancy and Theron were on the dance floor executing such a smooth two-step that it was fluid beauty.

"They should go on that dance thing on television," Sophie said.

"Who?" Elijah asked.

"Fancy and Theron. Watch them. They are really good together."

"Eat up, darlin', and we'll beat them all to pieces," Elijah said.

"You dance? You're kidding me," she said.

"No, ma'am. Jones boys have rhythm. Look at Tanner out there with that tall blonde. And he's the clumsy one in the family," Elijah said.

She located Tanner and his partner on the floor, and they were indeed every bit as graceful as Fancy and Theron. Her hands went sweaty at the prospect of dancing with Elijah. She hadn't been on the dance floor since the sale the year before and then it was only to dance a couple of times with men who continually stepped on her toes. Her husband had hated to dance, had absolutely no rhythm for dancing or singing. He couldn't carry a tune in a bucket with the lid welded tight, and had three left feet on the dance floor. The only time he'd ever waltzed her around the floor was the day they got married, and that was only for the first minute of the song and just to satisfy his obligation. Charisma poured from his pores when he talked, and he could preach a sermon that would bring a die-hard sinner to his knees. But he couldn't dance, and Sophie loved to dance.

When they finished their meal, Elijah pushed back his chair and said, "Miz Sophie, may I have this dance?"

She let him lead her to the dance floor and noticed when he nodded at the singer. "What is going on?" she whispered.

The lead singer finished his song and then leaned close to the microphone. "I've been told that this has been a good day for the ranch. The sale was beyond expectations and now the owners, Elijah Jones and Sophie McSwain, are going to dance to 'Cowboys and Angels,' an old Garth Brooks tune."

Elijah drew Sophie into his arms. She put one hand in his and an arm around his neck. From his first step, she was lost in the song and in the flawless execution of the finest two-steppin' she'd ever known. Elijah sang with Garth, his breath and the words of the song sending multicolored sparks floating around them like Independence Day fireworks.

Elijah and Garth sang about a cowboy who was stubborn and proud, reckless and loud, and how God noticed he'd never make it on his own. So God took thunder and passion, patience and wonder, and sent down the best thing that He'd ever made.

"That's me," Elijah whispered. "I've been proud and reckless and stubborn and loud, Sophie."

"Well, I'm low on patience, but I am also full of thunder and passion," she answered.

Elijah chuckled and went on to sing about cowboys and lace and about how salt of the earth met heavenly grace. "You are a sight to behold tonight in that lace. I'd believe you were an angel if it weren't for that Irish temper."

She smiled. "Darlin', you are a cowboy, but I do not have wings, and if I had a halo, it would be bent all to the devil and twisted up into a pretzel. I'm not an angel."

The song ended, and the whole barn erupted into applause. Elijah held Sophie's hand, and they took a deep bow. Then with a twinkle in her light gray eyes, Sophie turned around and said something to the singer. He nodded and leaned into the microphone.

"Seems Miz Sophie has a request. Let's see if the cowboy Garth was singing about can keep up with the angel in lace with this song. Give us a little bit of 'Country Girl' by Mr. Jason Aldean, boys."

The steel guitar and the drums started and Elijah's face lit up. Sophie played the part, shaking her finger out across the dance floor at everyone when the singer started off by asking if the boys had ever met a real country girl.

The music was loud and fast. Elijah grabbed her hand and followed her lead as she started something between an Irish reel and a fast line dance. He grinned when the singer said the girl was country from her "cowboy boots to her down home roots" and talked about her thick southern drawl, her sexy swing and walk. Neither of them missed a single beat, and when the song ended they were both panting.

"Great Scott, or maybe I should say Irish, I've never seen her dance like that," Fancy said.

"It's Elijah. He's her life after wife. She just don't know it yet," Kate said.

"And now I'm going to put our hosts through one more song before I let them leave the floor. Y'all give it up for the best dancers I've seen. Wow! These two could bring down the house at that dancing show on television. Hey, that's not giving it up. Y'all can do better than that," the singer said.

The night had been slow up until then, but now everyone was getting fired up and ready to dance, and a band liked a lively audience.

Applause echoed in the barn until Sophie thought the roof would lift.

"OK, let's have a little bit of Anthony Smith singing 'If That Ain't Country.'"

Elijah took a deep breath and got ready for another fast song. Sophie backed up to him and put both arms up over her head and around his neck. When the guitars whined and the singer started singing about a girl growing up out in the sticks where the ginseng grows, Sophie flipped around, switched her skirts back and forth, and the dancing began. The singer said the girl had a Bible, she'd been born again, she had a shotgun, and she wasn't afraid of sin.

By the time the dance ended, Elijah was laughing so hard he had trouble keeping in step, and Sophie was improvising, trying to throw him off his game. It ended with twanging guitars and drums and the guests didn't have to be told again to applaud.

"Y'all come on out here on the dance floor now that our hosts have broken the ice and let's have some fun," the singer said.

In minutes the floor was packed with Theron and Fancy leading the stampede.

"I'm dying for a cold beer," Sophie said.

"Oh, yeah!" he said.

"I do have a Bible and I do have a shotgun. You might do well to remember that," she said as he led her to the open bar and ordered two longneck Coors.

"Yes, ma'am. And do you have a moonshine still out behind the shed?" Elijah asked.

"No. Not yet," she teased.

He downed a whole glass of Dr Pepper and handed it back to the caterer for a refill. "That was more fun than I've had in years, Sophie. Thank you!"

"It warmed up the crowd. Look at that. Myrle even has someone out there with her," she motioned with her bottle toward the floor.

"Not doin' too bad but none of them can outdo us," Elijah said.

"It's been a good day and a wonderful party. To us." She clinked her bottle with his.

"To us," he repeated.

And for the first time, Elijah wanted more than a business relationship. He wanted much, much more and he wanted it with Sophie.

CHAPTER THIRTEEN

Sophie awoke slowly, opening her eyes, checking the clock to see that it was nine o'clock, hearing the noise of pots and pans in the kitchen, and smelling coffee and bacon. She stretched and then frowned. So many voices, all male, were coming from the kitchen. Was that Gus?

He didn't come to the ranch on Sunday. That was his day off. Had something happened? Was there another fire? She was out of the bed in a flash and stomping her feet down into her boots. She didn't have time to get dressed if there was another wildfire.

Boot heels on the hardwood floor in the hallway sounded like off-beat drum rolls, and she was out of breath when she reached the kitchen.

"Where's the fire?" Gus asked.

"That's what I was going to ask you." Sophie panted.

"No fire around here and it's raining. Can't ask for no better news than a great sale, a good party, and then rain the next day," Gus said.

Sophie melted into a kitchen chair across the table from Elijah. Hayden sat on one side of him, with Gus at one end of the table and Tanner at the other. They'd finished breakfast, but there was a big piece of paper stretched out on the table with diagrams and writing all over it.

Elijah pushed back his chair and ambled over to the cabinet, where he poured a cup of coffee for Sophie, then brought the pot to the table to refill everyone else's cups.

"Thank you, Elijah. What's going on? And why are you here?" Sophie looked at Gus.

"We've got a proposal to put before you," Elijah said. "But don't crawl up on that high horse of yours before you even hear us out. I didn't want to mention it until after the sale because you had enough on your mind. You go first, Gus."

Gus sipped his coffee and laid a hand on Sophie's. "I'll be eighty years old on my next birthday. It's way past time for me to retire. Me and the wife want to do a little bit of traveling before I bite the dust. So yesterday was my last day, darlin'. The ranch don't need me now that Elijah is here."

Tears filled Sophie's eyes. "The ranch will always need you."

"Now that's a right sweet thing for you to say. Miz Maud left me that right nice chunk of money in her will, and I want to spend some of it. You and Elijah are going to do right well here. That sale proved it to me, and I'd planned on leaving soon as she was gone, but I wanted to stick around until y'all got your ranchin' legs down strong. You've done it, and it's time for me to spend some time in my rockin' chair," Gus said.

"If you don't work, you'll get stiff with arthritis and die," Sophie said.

Gus laughed. "I don't reckon the wife is going to let that happen. She's got a list of honey-dos lined up that'll keep me from gettin' arthritis for a hun'erd years. Now give this old man a hug, and then I'm goin' to walk out of here. No tears.

No big foo-rah. Just a wonderful day to go home and sit on my porch and enjoy a fine rainy mornin'."

He and Sophie stood up at the same time and she hugged him fiercely.

Gus whispered softly in her ear, "Listen to these boys. They're scared to death you're goin' to say no, and it's a good plan. Your money ain't doin' you a bit of good drawin' the interest in the bank."

"I'll miss you so much," she said.

"And I reckon I'll miss the ranch, but it's time for me to step down. Like I said, Elijah is doing a fine job and, with you to partner with, the two of you are going to make this place into something really big. Maud and Jesse would be proud." He picked up his hat from the back of his chair, crammed it down on his head, and left as if he were going out to check on the cattle.

Sophie brushed a tear from her cheek and sat back down at the table. "What's with the paper?" she asked.

Hayden combed his dark hair with his fingers and looked over at Elijah.

"It's like this," Elijah started. "First of all, before I show you the map, let me explain about Hayden and Tanner."

"Hayden isn't going to teach next year, and Tanner's job disappeared when the cotton farmer sold out," she said.

"That's right." Elijah nodded seriously. "So they are both available to work for us."

"But we have Frankie, Kendall, and Randy all ready in the bunkhouse," she said.

"Yes, we do and there's room for three more out there. The two ranches south of us took a severe hit with the fire. The one right next to us was an abandoned house, and the people who own it were leasing it to the folks south of them. Those people suffered the biggest damage. They got their cattle out just fine, but their house and barn didn't survive. So they called me the morning of the sale to see if we'd be interested in buying since we have connecting land. The folks between us whose land they were leasing are looking to sell also. Our ranch is this section of land." He pointed to the map. "The next section is right here. That would be the Garretts' place. You said you had enough to buy me out, and I have enough to buy you out. What if you bought one of these sections, and I bought the other one. We'd triple the size of the ranch that way. We could run more cattle, get into the hay production in a bigger way, and make a lot more money."

She looked at the map on the table and remembered what Gus had whispered to her moments before. Could she really take a step that big? Did she trust Elijah enough to pool her money with his? What would she lose if she decided she could not work with the man after all?

She stared at the chart. "How much money are we talking about?"

Elijah pointed at the property due south of them. "These folks want seven fifty an acre if we'll take it all. This one wants eight an acre. A square mile or six hundred forty acres in each deal.

Sophie did the math in her head. "Just under a million for both sections."

"Closing costs and lawyer fees would make it pretty close to the whole mil," Elijah said. "I'll put in half if you will. Then we can share the cost of more equipment to get the place up and running by spring time."

It felt right, but that was a lot of money.

"Can I think about it?"

"The sellers are putting it on the market in a week if we don't give them an answer," Elijah told her.

"We wanted to buy into the proposition, but Elijah said that two bosses were enough," Hayden said.

"Most of the time it's one too many." Sophie tried to smile, but those big dollar signs kept dancing around in her head in bright neon colors.

"Hungry?" Elijah asked.

"Starving," Sophie answered.

"Think maybe a western omelet and half a dozen strips of bacon might help you think about it harder?" he asked.

She nodded. "Would we keep the brand the same?"

I tried to buy that land for years, and if you don't do this, I'm going to sit on the side of your bed every night and pester the living daylights out of you, Aunt Maud's voice was suddenly inside her head. *It's a wonderful plan, and you've got money just molding away in that savings account. If you don't like it in a year, then sell out to Elijah. And by the way, I loved the party last night. I knew that if you two were pitched into a sinking ship, you'd figure out how to paddle it to shore. Now buy the land! It's a precious commodity. Ain't no more bein' made on the earth, so buy what you can, when you can.*

"You can make that decision. I got no problem with the Double Bar M brand." Elijah pushed his chair back and headed to the stove. All the makings for omelets were still lined up, so he broke three eggs into a bowl, popped two pieces of bread into the toaster, and, without wasting a single motion, had an omelet prepared and toast buttered in record time.

"Thank you, and OK, let's do it," Sophie said when he set the plate in front of her.

"That all the time you need?" Elijah was amazed.

She nodded. "It feels right."

She didn't tell him that the money she received from her husband's insurance policy had never been touched, or that her half of the venture would only use up a small portion of what was in the bank.

Hayden and Tanner slapped hands in a high five and then grabbed Sophie in a sandwich hug. Sophie giggled and wiggled free.

"Mercy." She gasped. "I didn't see that coming."

Hayden grinned. "OK, then we move into the bunkhouse today. If we're out by eleven, we won't have to pay another motel day, and we'll be ready for work tomorrow morning."

Sophie nodded as she stuffed a forkful of eggs, flavored with peppers, cheese, and bacon, into her mouth. It seemed a lifetime ago since she'd put on her black suit to wear to Aunt Maud's funeral. How could so much happen in a month's time? The future loomed before her and it didn't look so scary. She'd made a major decision without shaking in her boots, and she could almost hear Aunt Maud giggling behind her.

Hayden and Tanner threw back the rest of their coffee and stood at the same time. "See y'all in half an hour. Where do we stow our extra stuff?"

Sophie looked up with a question on her face.

"We came to beg for a job, so we came ready to stay. Figured we could haul it all back home better than we could make a five-hour trip to get it if y'all said you could use our help," Tanner said.

"How much extra stuff?"

"Don't know until we see the bunkhouse. We'll keep as much as we can out there," Hayden said.

"Use the balcony in the sale barn," Elijah said. "It won't be used again until next year. By then maybe we'll have some other living arrangements in order."

Sophie cut her eyes around at him.

"Don't look at me like that. I've got lots of plans, and we can discuss them now or later," he said.

"Right now!" she said and motioned for him to sit down.

Hayden and Tanner made a hasty retreat outside, leaving Elijah and Sophie to fight about whatever plans he had already made without talking to her first.

"OK, spit it out," she said.

"This week's or this month's worth of plans?" Elijah asked.

Sophie rolled her gray eyes at him. "Start with this week and proceed from there."

"How long you got?"

"It's nine thirty. I reckon I've got about twelve or thirteen hours. That long enough? If not I could stay awake until midnight."

He grinned.

"If it's going to take longer than that, then talk fast." She set into the rest of the omelet before it got really cold.

"OK, this week, tomorrow, we take their offer unless you think we should counterbid and start negotiations."

She shrugged. "The price is fair. The ranch I tried to buy to get you off the Double Bar M was a thousand dollars an acre. It did have a house, but it also had lots more mesquite to deal with."

Elijah raised an eyebrow. "So you tried to kick me off for a ranch of chiggers and mesquite?"

"Nothing ventured, nothing gained. You didn't budge, did you? We going to argue or plan?" she asked.

Elijah glared at her.

She glared back.

He chuckled.

Her eyes twinkled.

"OK, so neither of us is budging. You got any dreams about this ranch?" he asked.

Her head slowly went from side to side. "Not one thing. Just figured I'd keep on doing what Aunt Maud did, but I reckon it's either grow or get swallowed up, ain't it?"

"That's the truth in a nutshell. I'd kind of figured the same way when she wrote and said she was leaving me half the ranch," Elijah said.

Sophie held up a palm. "Whoa, partner! She left you the ranch?"

"Well, yes. It certainly didn't come from Santa Claus or the Easter Bunny."

"I thought Uncle Jesse wanted you to have half."

"He did, but he left the actual doing of it up to Aunt Maud."

You sneaky devil, Sophie thought. *Where are you right now? You were all ready to give me advice a while ago but now you are silent? Did you think I'd never find out that you deliberately brought this man onto the Double Bar M? What in the devil were you thinking, Aunt Maud?*

But Aunt Maud must have been off in a corner somewhere telling St. Peter all about cattle ranching in Texas because she didn't have a thing to say to Sophie.

"So," Elijah went on. "According to our bank records, we have enough to buy two more tractors this fall. Both of those places already have steel fence posts, so we just have to take care of that around our original land. I figure our original crew can put up new fencing, and Hayden and Tanner can begin to clear off what mesquite didn't burn and get the other two sections ready for a winter wheat crop. As we have time, you and I can begin to hit the sales and buy some new blood for the cattle line."

Sophie looked at the figures he had written on the edge of the paper. They looked solid. He'd left a healthy account in the bank in case of disaster. A good rancher never used up everything down to the last penny or else something would come along and he'd have to start borrowing. And Aunt Maud said that was the downfall of the small-time rancher.

"Used or brand new?" she asked.

"We talkin' cattle or tractors?"

"You know exactly what I'm talkin' about. First rattle out of the bucket has to be tractors. If we don't have land to graze the new stock, then we might as well not buy them."

"Used. There's a sale over in Abilene on Friday night. Auction on a couple of ranches that are selling out. I saw the sale bill in the Dairy Queen, and Theron mentioned it yesterday. They've got a couple of John Deeres that look good, and Theron thinks they'll go for a reasonable price. They're also offering a really good used Dodge Ram truck that's only three years old with good mileage that I thought I'd buy, but that's personal, not ranch money."

"OK, now go on," she said.

"You going with me to the sale?"

"Well, I'm not staying home," she declared. "You might not buy the right tractors, and besides, there might be something else for sale that we'll need, like rakes and plows."

"It starts at eight o'clock," he said.

"Then I suppose we'd better get up early."

"My long-term plan is that we'll make money on this, take out a modest paycheck like we give the guys, plow the rest of the profits back into the ranch, buy some more land that adjoins us as it comes up for sale, run more cattle, and hire more help along the way. And eventually build a couple of houses out on the new property."

He waited for her to catch up.

"One for Hayden and one for Tanner so they'll stay close by?" she asked.

"Man likes to have some family around," he answered.

"You've been pretty busy this past month," she said.

"I just see an opportunity here to expand, to make a good living, and to help a lot of people out at the same time. In ten years, we'll be running an operation with a payroll of maybe a hundred people."

"Whoa, cowboy! Are you serious?"

He nodded. "Yes, I am. Two sections this year, Sophie. Maybe one a year after that from the profits. It's going to snowball, and pretty soon we'll have the biggest spread in all of central Texas."

She giggled. "Dream big if you want. But don't ever ask me to go into debt."

"No, ma'am. Aunt Maud and Uncle Jesse didn't borrow against the land. We won't either," Elijah said.

"You got anything else to say?"

He reached across the table and took both her hands in his. "Just thank you."

Every nerve in her body tingled at his touch. She wanted to pull her hands away before they burned into nothing but a pile of ashes right there on their future plans, but she could not. She and Elijah had just set out their future right there at the kitchen table, but she had no idea if it was totally business or if there was room for something personal, even though it wasn't written on the paper.

"Let's ride my motorcycle down to Baird and have some ice cream to celebrate," he said softly.

"I've never ridden a cycle and besides it's raining," she said.

"Then, honey, you are in for a surprise. And the rain is just passing through. It'll be gone in an hour. It'll take us that long to finish another cup of coffee, talk some more about how much winter wheat to plant for grazing after we plow under the ashes, and for you to get ready."

CHAPTER FOURTEEN

The morning had that fresh, new quality that comes after a big decision is reached and after a lot of work has been done. Steam rose off the ground as the hot sunrays reclaimed what moisture they could before it sunk into the dirt. A fresh, clean scent in the air mixed with excitement over riding a motorcycle for the very first time. Sophie had tucked a T-shirt into a pair of jeans, put on her work cowboy boots, and pulled her red hair back into a ponytail. When she heard the powerful Harley engine grumbling around the house to the front yard, she forgot about makeup and hurried through the house and outside.

It wasn't her first date and it couldn't really be classified as a date. But she was giddier than she'd been that first time when she was sixteen and went to the junior prom with Mitchell O'Malley. She kept telling herself that she was not a sophomore in high school; she was thirty-one years old and this was just a ride to Baird for ice cream.

It didn't work. When she saw the motorcycle parked in the yard with Elijah waiting in his tight jeans, black T-shirt, and boots, her heart fluttered around like a butterfly fighting against the wind.

"Ready?" he asked.

She nodded, unable to utter a single word.

He handed her a shiny black helmet. "Better put this on."

She crammed it down on her head and fumbled with the chin strap. He reached out and fastened it for her, then flipped the clear face guard down. His touch on the soft part of her neck did nothing to calm her already racing heart.

"Crawl on behind me and put your arms around my waist."

She threw a long leg over the cycle and settled into the seat.

He grabbed both her hands and planted them firmly around his waist, revved up the engine, and they were on their way. Before they reached the end of the lane and turned west to the highway, she was in love. Every doubt or fear that she'd had about buying the land disappeared right along with all the bitterness of the past. When he turned onto the highway and headed south toward town, he picked up speed. Sophie felt like she was a butterfly, flying away from everything that had held her back, leaving nothing but the beautiful smell of rain and wind rushing against her skin.

She wished it was a hundred miles to the Dairy Queen, but it was only a ten-minute ride. Disappointment crept into her soul when he parked the bike, took off his helmet, and helped her remove hers. After he'd hung them on the handlebars, he offered a hand to help her off the bike.

How could a big old callused hand wrapped around hers cause such a reaction? She wondered this as he laced his fingers in hers, with his thumb making lazy circles on the top of her hand. There were few people in the Dairy Queen: one table of coffee drinkers in the back corner, old men in overalls discussing politics loudly, and two young girls poring over a catalog in a booth, giggling and pointing at items before turning the pages.

The scent of sausage and bacon from the breakfast run still permeated the air. Sophie heard the sizzle of hamburgers hitting the grill and smelled onions.

"What can I get you folks? Breakfast is already over so you'll have to order from the lunch menu," a middle-aged woman said from behind the counter.

"I want a banana split with whipped cream and nuts," Elijah said.

"Make that two," Sophie added. It was a heck of a lot of calories and fat grams, but if she was going to work three square miles of land, she'd soon shake it all off. Besides, today was celebration day. They'd had an awesome sale and hired two more hands to help and Gus had retired. The latter threatened tears, but she kept them at bay. She'd be happy for Gus, not sad. He deserved a few years to sit in his rocking chair on the porch between the honey-do things his wife had in store.

Elijah paid the lady with a bill and told her to keep the change. He led Sophie back to a booth and dropped her hand when they sat down on opposite sides. "So what do you think?"

"I'll have to walk twenty miles to work off all the calories I'm about to eat, and that's not even taking into account that enormous omelet and toast I had this morning," she said.

"Not that. The motorcycle," he said.

"I loved it Elijah. It's…it's…there're no words to describe it. It's freedom and laughter and butterfly wings all tied up together with a red bow," she gushed.

He laughed. "I've never heard it called that. I guess I'll keep it if you like it that much."

Her eyes popped open so wide that they hurt. "You were going to sell it?"

"Thought about it, but if you like it we'll keep it for Sunday afternoon rides so you can have your freedom and butterflies." He chuckled again.

"Thank you, but if you ever decide to sell it, I'll buy the rascal. Just name your price," she said.

The waitress set two banana splits on the table. Sophie picked up the plastic spoon and dipped into the end with the chocolate topping. "Mmmm," she said.

Elijah did the same. "Good!"

"Not as good as the ride but still wonderful," she said between bites.

"When we finish, you want a longer ride?"

A brilliant smile lit up her face. "Where to?"

"Ever been to Fort Griffin?"

"Not since I went there as a kid on a school field trip."

"It's about a forty-five-minute drive up there. I heard that they were rebuilding the old jail and putting up a general store."

"Aunt Maud said that someone was plowing a bunch of money into the old place, keeping it as historical as possible."

"Guess we'd best go check on it and see if it meets our approval."

She giggled. "As if the historical society cares what we think. I didn't get a letter asking if I agreed with them rebuilding the old jail. Did you?"

"Of course I did. It had the official state seal of Texas on it and the whole nine yards. Could be that I'm a decorated war vet and they want my opinion on such things whereas you are just a ranchin' woman," he teased.

Sophie shook her spoon at him. "Do not underestimate the powers of a cattle woman."

"Wouldn't dream of it," he said.

"What did you do in the war, Elijah?"

"That would be Eli, ma'am. And I could tell you but then…" He left the age-old line hanging.

"I like Elijah better, and you'd better bring an army if you ever want to kill me. One man ain't big enough." She flirted back at him and it felt good.

"Oh?" He raised both dark eyebrows.

"That's right, buster. I'm a tough woman like Aunt Maud. She bequeathed me half her ranch and all her sass. So stand aside if you think you can run over me."

"Wouldn't dream of it, not if she left you all her mean! Uncle Jesse used to say that she was ninety percent bluff and only ten percent mean, but no one wanted to test her mettle because that ten percent was deadly if she had to drag it out."

Sophie leaned across the table and whispered, "He was a very smart man, and I got all of mine now plus hers."

"Well then, sassy woman, eat your ice cream before it all melts, and we'll go stomp around the old fort and work off the calories. You like to hike?"

Sophie shrugged. "I like outside."

"You never been hiking?" he asked.

She shrugged again. "What's the formal definition of 'hiking'? I've been out walking in the pastures and sometimes in the woods."

"I'll take you on a real hike sometime and you can see for yourself. How about fishing?"

She nodded. "Boring! Went with my dad when I was a kid a couple of times."

"Out to a farm pond?"

"That's right."

"I'll take you real fishing, in a boat out on a lake with the sun and wind."

"Promise?"

"Sure, next Sunday we'll ride the bike up to Breckenridge to the lake and rent a boat. You know how to cook catfish or bass?"

She shook her head. "Love it but never cooked it."

"Then I'll do the cookin' if we catch anything."

She pushed the clear plastic boat to the middle of the table. "My eyes were bigger than my stomach. I should've ordered a sundae. Help me finish the last scoop. Butterscotch is my least favorite of the three toppings."

"It's my favorite. I love butterscotch pie, too, but seldom find it in the restaurants. Piecrust is not my specialty. When I make it, it's like shoe leather."

He stuck his spoon deeply into the ice cream.

She did the same.

Sharing the banana split with him was sealing their partnership forever. They'd do just fine in the cattle business. Elijah had vision and purpose, and she appreciated that in him.

❖ ❖ ❖

Elijah hadn't meant to keep her hand in his when he helped her off the motorcycle, but it felt good and she didn't jerk hers away. He'd never known a woman like Sophie McSwain. Any other woman would have crumbled when she discovered her preacher husband was nothing but a glory-seeking cheater, but not Sophie. She held her head up, started all over in Baird, Texas, with Aunt Maud to guide her, and that had made her a stronger woman.

They had a battle of spoons over the last bit of butterscotch syrup. They were still laughing about who got the last drop as they left the Dairy Queen and mounted up to ride north. He'd ridden for years, had his first cycle when he was sixteen, and upgraded it every time he could until he had the Harley of his dreams. But seeing the world through Sophie's eyes that warm September morning was a whole new vision. One that he liked very much.

It was a little over forty miles up to Fort Griffin, then another mile or so back down a winding, narrow road to the visitor's center. They passed longhorn cattle weaving in and out among the mesquite. Big brindle bulls, spotted cows, and even a few calves bawling for their mommas when the big evil-looking machine shot past them.

The sun was high in the sky and pouring down enough heat that, when Elijah parked the cycle, sweat had moistened Sophie's hair, making it kink up even tighter. She pulled the rubber band from the ponytail and shook her head. Red ringlets fell to her shoulders.

"Looks like you went swimming." Elijah smiled.

"Yours is wet, too."

"I like yours down and curly like that," Elijah whispered.

"I like yours long and in a ponytail."

He vowed that he wouldn't cut it again, not even for the sale. He put a hand on the small of her back and guided her into the visitor's center, where he pulled out a ten-dollar bill to pay the admittance fee. She hurried on past the clerk's station to the restroom. Elijah pocketed the change and looked around at the postcards, brochures, and souvenirs offered in the small store while he waited on Sophie. He bought a keychain with a set of silver longhorns dangling from it and shoved it down in his pocket. When she came out, he grabbed her hand again and they were off to explore.

❖ ❖ ❖

Sophie looked out across the rolling hills and tried to imagine the days when Fort Griffin and The Flat, which was the town situated between the fort and the Clear Fork of the Brazos River, was in full operation. It was billed as a place so rough that even the army left. She didn't have a bit of trouble visualizing a place that rough and tumble back in 1860, right before the Civil War.

"I read up about this place on the Internet. Seems it had the reputation for being one of the most lawless communities in the state. It was here before Shackelford County was even formed, so there wasn't any law except for the military," Elijah said.

"You like military history?" she asked.

"Oh, yeah! I'm standing here trying to picture exactly what it would have been like back then when Pat Garrett, Doc Holliday, and Wyatt Earp rolled into The Flat and tangled with Lottie Deno, Big Nose Kate, and John Wesley Hardin." He waved out across the mesquite and scrub oak dotting the hills.

"Me, too. Today you are Doc Holliday, and I'm the schoolmarm. Let's go take a look at The Flat and go back in time." She grabbed his hand and pulled him toward the walking trail that led down over the hill into a flat area that housed the town more than a hundred years before.

She stopped at the jail and said, "OK, Doc, tell me something. This jail isn't much bigger than my bedroom. What in the world did you do when there was a real saloon brawl and you had a dozen men to lock up?"

"Why, Miz Sophie, we threw them all in there together. We didn't care if they had to sleep standin' up. In those days there was no prisoner's rights. They gave up their rights when they disobeyed the law. Maybe if they didn't smell too pretty or had to stand right next to the fellow that they'd been hittin' on, they'd think twice about startin' a fight next time."

She smiled and shuddered when she touched the stone walls of the jail. It had no windows and the ceiling was barely high enough for her to stand up inside. A six-foot buffalo hunter would have to sit or keep his neck bent at a terribly uncomfortable angle if he wanted to stand.

"Over here, right next door, is the saloon," Elijah said.

"You ever been in there, Doc?" Sophie kept the game going.

"Yes, ma'am. They served some good cold brew in there, and my presence kept the fights down some of the time. Between me and Wyatt and Pat, we could maintain a little bit of order. It helped if we were right out there among the people, our badges all shiny and flashing, instead of sitting behind a desk," Elijah answered.

"And the place where I could buy staples is right next door." She wiggled her fingers free from his and sat down on the wooden bench in front of the store. The general store and the saloon were one rough wood building. The saloon had a peak roof and the general store a tiny little three-step facade, but they shared the porch. If she shut her eyes tightly, she could imagine bawdy piano music and the smell of ale coming from the saloon. She could see women in long skirts choosing fabric for a new dress and embroidery threads from the general store while their husbands had a brew next door. She could see buffalo in the distance and soldiers coming and going from the fort up on the hill.

Elijah crooked his arm and she stood up, slipped hers in it, and they continued on to the blacksmith shop. Another rough wood building with four posts, barely scraped clean of bark, holding up the slanted porch roof. In her mind it was busy and hot, with a raging fire going in a pit so the blacksmith could soften the metals before he beat them into shape. She could hear the ting of the ball-peen hammer and feel the heat finding its way out into the yard.

"What are you thinking about?" Elijah asked.

"I'm picturing it all in my mind. Would you have wanted to ride with Pat Garrett and Wyatt Earp?" she asked.

"What makes you think I would have been on that side of the law?" He chuckled.

She slapped his arm softly. "Elijah Jones, even in another era, you would have been the cowboy in the white hat."

He smiled. "Why thank you, Miz Sophie. I appreciate your confidence. But I might have been the blacksmith or the general store owner."

"Nope. You might have been the commander of the fort if you hadn't been a lawman."

"You got a higher opinion of me today than you did a month ago at the funeral," he said.

"Today, darlin', you've got a higher opinion of me, too. Would you have offered to let me buy half those ranches a month ago? I don't think so. You would have bought them and tried to wear me down to sell my half of the Double Bar M."

They walked back to the two-story building that now housed the Fort Griffin Lodge Hall. The historical marker outside said that it was chartered in 1878. Less than ten years later, the US Army vacated Fort Griffin and the Texas Central Railway bypassed the town. The lodge moved to Throckmorton, but school was held in the building until 1937.

"So this was your building, Miz Sophie," Elijah said.

"Yes, we had a potbellied stove over there and long lines of desks with a center aisle so I could walk up and down to check my students' work. I had the soldiers' kids, the town kids, and even the children who were born to the ladies who worked for Big Nose Kate. They were a diverse group, but kids are kids. They learned, they grew up, and they left the school," she said.

"You ever want to be a school teacher?" Elijah asked.

She shook her head. "But standing here and thinking about the primitive methods they used, I think I might have liked it back then."

When they were back outside, they found another historical marker. It mentioned a newspaper called the *Fort Griffin Echo*. Sophie ran her hand over the raised lettering and asked, "If you weren't a commander or a lawman, maybe you'd have been a newspaper man."

He laughed. "Not me. I'm too controversial for that. I'd make someone mad enough to hang me in every single edition."

"That's the truth," she agreed.

"So have we worked off our ice cream? You ready for a midafternoon late lunch or early supper?" he asked.

"Where you thinkin' about?"

"The Eagle's Nest in Albany. Church crew will be finished and gone. We'd probably have the place to ourselves, and they make a pretty good chicken fried steak," he said.

Her stomach growled loudly as they headed up the hill toward the visitor's center.

"Guess I got my answer." He laughed.

"Chicken fried steak does sound good."

Elijah stopped and looked down into her eyes. "Why aren't you at the girls' powwow today?"

"It's not set in stone that we get together every single Sunday afternoon, but we do try. Today Kate has to be off at a family gathering with Hart, and Theron's parents came to visit from Shamrock, so Fancy Lynn is busy with family, too."

"What about next Sunday when we go fishing?"

"It's on the way. I'll spend half an hour with them and meet you at the lake," she said.

"How about if I holler at Theron and we do something for an hour, and that way we can still ride the cycle together?"

"Sounds like a plan." She picked up the helmet, crammed it down on her head, and mounted the back seat of the big bike. When Elijah crawled on she wrapped her arms around him and was amazed anew at the tingly feeling that danced up and down her backbone.

It only took fifteen minutes to reach the café in Albany and it was empty. They sat at a table near a window, and the waitress came right away with two tall glasses of ice water.

Elijah waved away the menus and told her they'd have two glasses of sweet tea and two of the chicken fried steak dinners. "I want ranch dressing on my salad. What about you, Sophie?"

"Honey mustard," she said.

The waitress nodded and disappeared back into the kitchen.

"You grew up in this town. Did y'all hang out here all the time?" He looked around at the bulletin board with pictures of that year's football team and the schedule.

"Not us. We weren't the popular kids, Elijah. We were just barely considered middle class, and we sure don't have any football queen tiaras in our memory boxes. We all left the area when we were fifteen. Fancy Lynn's momma got remarried and they moved to Florida since her stepdad was a career military man and stationed there. My dad got a promotion in the oil company and we moved out to the Texas Panhandle, from there to Cushing, Oklahoma, and then to Alma, Arkansas. I went to school at the university in Fayetteville. Kate's dad went back to the sugar plantation down in Louisiana."

"And you kept in touch all those years?" he asked.

The waitress brought their tea and set it on the table, along with their salads and a basket of assorted crackers.

Sophie shoved a mouthful of lettuce and tomatoes in her mouth. She hadn't realized how hungry she was until she sat down and smelled the aroma of food wafting from the kitchen.

"Oh yeah," she said when she swallowed and took a sip of tea. "There were letters, then phone calls, then cell phone calls and texting, and then we were back in the area all within a year."

"I never had lifelong friends like that. I've got military buddies that might come see me sometime, and of course my brothers. I've always been closer to Hayden and Tanner than the four older boys."

"Isn't there one closer to your age?"

Elijah nodded. "Noah is closer to me in age. He's married. Has four kids. He did not take to ranchin'."

"A Jones that doesn't like dirt and cows? You sure your folks didn't find him in a bar ditch along side of the road and just take him in?" she teased.

He chuckled. "That's exactly what we told him all those years growing up. He hated to go outside, would rather stay in the house and help Momma or else read a book. It wasn't a surprise when he told us he was going into the ministry."

The waitress brought their steaks at the very moment they'd finished their salads, set the plates in front of them, refilled their tea, and disappeared again.

"Very good," Elijah said after the first bite.

They settled right into their food, the silence between them as comfortable as the hiking at Fort Griffin and the ice cream in Baird. It all felt right and that scared Elijah, who had a sudden case of "what ifs" with every bite.

Sophie hated to get off the bike at the ranch when they returned, but it was time to do chores. Check the cattle, feed the chickens, take care of the dogs and cats, and make sure Hayden and Tanner had gotten moved in. They'd already been working with the other three hired hands during the sale, so everyone was acquainted.

She hung the helmet back on the handlebars and sighed. The day had come to an end too quickly. If Elijah had offered to ride all the way to the Pacific Ocean, she would have been game. Tanner could take on the job of foreman immediately and run the ranch for a couple of weeks. But Elijah was slinging a leg off the bike and plucking his helmet from his head, strands of hair sticking to his forehead.

"Well?" he said.

"What?"

"Still up for another trip next Sunday and some serious fishing?"

"Already looking forward to it. Don't suppose we could take it to the sale on Friday, could we?"

"No, because if I buy that truck, I'll need you to drive our ranch truck back home."

Two words stood out and made those butterflies start two-stepping around in her heart again: "our" and "home." She liked the way they sounded.

She started for the porch. Her boot sunk into a gopher hole right beside the first step and she fell backward. One minute her feet were firmly on the ground even though her head was in the clouds. The next she was falling in slow motion and then strong arms were holding her tightly.

How she got turned around in his arms, facing him and plastered tight against his chest, she'd never figure out. But she would never forget the soft, dreamy way his eyes looked at her just before he kissed her, or the shocking electricity between them that lingered when he stepped back.

"Guess we'd best go in the house," he said hoarsely.

Her ringtone set up a howl in her shirt pocket. The old K. T. Oslin song let her know it was either Kate or Fancy. She walked around the end of the house and sat down under a shade tree before she answered it.

"Hello."

"It's Kate, and I was about to hang up."

"We just got back. I was angling for a shade tree before I answered it," Sophie said.

"Where have you been? I just met a whole raft of Ducaine cousins, and I'm about to set you up with a date for Friday night. Will it be Reed or Luther?"

"Neither."

"You promised, girl. After the sale, you promised if you didn't have a date, then me and Fancy get to set you up until you found your life after wife."

"I had a date, so you don't have to fix me up."

Well, it was a date. They'd gone out, had ice cream, which he paid for, went to a museum type thing, which he paid for, and then he paid for dinner, so that was a date by definition. And he'd even kissed her, so it went one step beyond definition.

"With who?"

"With whom," Sophie corrected her.

"You know exactly what I mean."

"With Elijah."

"Bull!"

"We went to Baird on his motorcycle for ice cream," Sophie went on with the details leaving out the kiss, "and the only bull I saw was a longhorn beauty up in Fort Griffin."

"I'll be hanged. Aunt Maud was right."

"Oh, no she wasn't! But I did have a date, and you and Fancy are free from your obligation. See you next Sunday."

"And you'd best bring details and lots of them," Kate said.

"I only have an hour because we are going fishing."

"Good grief. A man takes a woman fishing it's serious as sharing his hymn book in church. I'll get the wedding plans going."

"Don't you dare!" Sophie gasped.

Kate's laughter rang in her ears a full minute after she hung up.

CHAPTER FIFTEEN

The week went by like greased lightning. First there was a meeting with the lawyers over the sale, then the bank over the transfer of funds, and then signing enough papers that Sophie wondered if she was buying the whole state of Texas. While they were doing that, Hayden and Kendall were off checking prices on fencing and new barbed wire. When they found the place that would give them the best deal, they tallied up the total and brought the figures to the kitchen table.

Tanner supervised Frankie and Randy while the rest of the hands were busy, and they did chores, plowed and planted three hundred acres of winter wheat, and took care of the mundane everyday business of a ranch.

Come Thursday night all seven of them pulled chairs up around the kitchen table. Hayden reported that he and Kendall had bought and hauled in enough fencing to go around the whole original Double Bar M. Tanner reported what he'd gotten done with the cattle, and set up a date to work all the new calves. Tanner would be responsible for bringing the vaccinations from the feed store in Baird. Randy and Frankie would help with the branding and inoculations.

That left Hayden and Kendall to start replacing fence.

"We'll put up a mile of new and then take out the old. When you guys get the cattle worked you can help us. It should keep us out of jail for a month," Hayden said.

Frankie laughed. "At least through the week. Ain't makin' no promises about stayin' out of jail the weekend after payday."

"You get in jail once, I'll bail you out and dock your paycheck for the amount," Elijah said. "Twice and you can hunt for another job."

"Daddy's rules." Hayden smiled.

"That's right. They worked then and they'll work now if these boys want to have a job on the Double Bar M," Elijah said.

Frankie swallowed hard, his Adam's apple bobbing up and down. "Yes, sir."

"Daddy always had at least five hired hands besides us boys," Tanner said. "That was rule number one."

"What was number two?" Randy asked.

"No drinking on the job," all three brothers said in unison.

Elijah laid a hand on Randy's shoulder. "You drink on the job, you endanger your life and the partner you are working with. Drunk man can wreck a piece of machinery and kill himself, a dozen cows, and another hand. So no drinking on the job."

"Any other rules?" Kendall asked.

"Number three: no women in the bunkhouse," Hayden said.

"Not even for supper?" Kendall fired back.

"Supper is fine. Watchin' television is fine, but kiss 'em goodnight at the door and send them home. Weekends are yours to do whatever you please. And if you got the energy to chase skirts through the week after workin' all day, then have at it. You fall asleep on the job, you'll be lookin' for another one," Elijah said.

Suddenly Sophie was very glad she had a man to help her run the ranch. She'd never even thought about rules with the hired hands since Gus took care of all that.

"That all?" Randy asked.

"One more," Hayden said. "That is if we're going to run this like Daddy ran the cotton farm."

Elijah looked at him with a puzzled expression.

Hayden went on. "Saturday, at straight up noon, is payday. Miz Sophie will have your checks written out and ready when you come in to eat that day. You better be in the bunkhouse on Monday morning at six thirty for breakfast. In the case of an emergency, you've got Miz Sophie's cell phone number so call her. And that's the only reason you'll not be at the breakfast table, sober and ready for work on Monday morning. Anyone of you got a problem with the rules, or do I need to write them down and nail them to the wall in the bunkhouse?"

Everyone shook their heads.

"Then I expect we'd best get on about our jobs this morning. Soon as we get this fence up, we'll be doing a heck of a lot of plowing and planting. You'll be wishin' you could string barbed wire before we get more than a thousand acres ready for winter wheat."

Kendall rolled his eyes toward the ceiling. "We're going to get it all done this winter?"

"Nope, but we're not going to slow down," Hayden said. "We're going to fight mesquite until the Double Bar M is as clean as the cotton farms out in West Texas. Until our pastures are as green as Irish land and our cows are so fat that people beg us to sell to them. I expect you two" —Hayden looked at Elijah and Sophie— "had better go find us some equipment to work this big old patch of countryside. Two tractors ain't goin' to get much done, and we ain't seen a mule on the place."

Tanner shook his head. "Mules might be cheaper than tractors, even used ones."

"Yeah, but the production ain't as good, and I'd rather be ridin' in an air-conditioned cab as walkin' behind a mule all day," Kendall said.

Frankie slapped him on the shoulder. "How do you know? You ain't never looked at a mule's fanny all day long."

"Bet me? My grandpa had a two-acre garden and a stubborn old mule that took a fit every so often and wouldn't budge. And guess who got to plow that garden under every spring?" He pointed at his chest.

They were still topping each other's stories as they filed out the kitchen door and headed off to do their jobs that morning. Elijah looked over at Sophie and raised an eyebrow.

"We'll get them raised. It'll just take time," she teased.

"Well, if we expect to do a decent job with them we better go find them some new toys. Grab the ranch checkbook, and we'll see if those tractors are as good as the sale bill says they are," he said.

Sophie wore jeans with a Western-cut shirt hanging out over her belt, boots, and her best straw hat. She picked up her purse, made sure she had half a dozen checks in an envelope stashed in a side pocket and her cell phone charged up, and put on her sunglasses.

"I'm ready," she said.

"Good ranch woman," he said.

"And what is that supposed to mean?" she snapped at him.

"It means you are a good ranch woman. You know that we need to get to the sale and you're ready to go. I appreciate that."

"Good ranch man," she said.

"What's that supposed to mean?" He held the door open for her.

"It means you've got the good sense to know a good ranch woman when you see one."

"You sounded like Maud." He crossed the porch behind her and opened the pickup door. It wasn't as good as sitting on the cycle with her arms around his waist, but riding in the front seat side by side wasn't too bad.

"That, sir, is the best compliment you can pay me," she told him.

❖ ❖ ❖

Sophie didn't know a good tractor from a lemon. She did know that Aunt Maud liked John Deeres and they were green, but that was the extent of her knowledge on them. However, Elijah did not have to know that, now did he?

They arrived at the auction thirty minutes before starting time and circled the whole area. Elijah had the forethought to bring along a notepad, and he wrote down such things as hours the tractors had been used, if and when the engine had been overhauled, and what year it had been bought.

"What do you think?" Elijah asked.

"Honestly?"

"Of course."

"I don't know jack about a tractor. That was Gus and Aunt Maud's bailiwick. I was the accountant. I can drive a tractor and pull a plow or a baler behind it, but I wouldn't know a good one from a bad one." She wondered why she'd fessed up when she could have had him thinking she was so much smarter than he was.

It was the kisses. Aunt Maud was back in her head. *But it's a wise thing to be honest because then that puts him on the hot seat to be the same.*

Elijah nodded seriously. "OK, I'll confess that I'm pretty slow when it comes to accounting, so I'm glad you can do that. I don't have any idea what's tax deductible or what has to be depreciated out, or even how to do taxes or insurance forms."

"Guess we'll get along just fine then. Please tell me you know something about tractors," she said.

"I do. Daddy was adamant that all of his sons know equipment. And a cotton tractor is the same thing as an alfalfa or winter wheat tractor," he said. "The best one on the lot today is that one right there." He pointed to one with wheels almost as tall as Sophie. "Next best would be those two. I'd like to buy all three if the price is right."

"What about that little one over there?" She pointed at a small red one at the end of the lot.

"It's a good tractor but too small for much except making a garden. We going to plant a vegetable garden next spring?"

"Of course. Aunt Maud would sit on the bedpost and haunt me at night if we didn't plant our tomatoes, green beans, squash, and cantaloupes. We usually put in about a quarter of an acre and we canned what we didn't use. Won't be much cannin' goin' on with five big, strappin' men sitting at the supper table," she told him.

"That sounded like something Momma would have said. She said she had to have a garden to keep us out of the poorhouse with nine boys."

She frowned. "I remember that there're four older ones and then you and Noah, and the twins that we've inherited. But that's only eight," she said.

"You're leaving out Jedidiah. He's right under me in age. Thirty-eight last spring. He started off career military and then transferred into the FBI. Works out of Washington, DC, and comes home about once a year when my oldest brother and his wife host the annual family reunion at Thanksgiving. Never married except to his job."

"So you all weren't ranchers or farmers after all."

"Seven out of nine ain't too bad. Well, six out of nine, and then I came around to their way of thinking, thanks to Aunt Maud," Elijah said.

"Ladies and gentlemen, gather round and we'll get this show on the road," the auctioneer's big booming voice came through a sound system. "First thing we've got to offer is this trailer and everything on it. If you'll notice, there're tools in this box, fruit jars in that one, and lots of miscellaneous farm stuff in the rest of the boxes. Let's start the bidding at two hundred dollars."

Elijah raised his hand.

"I've got two, let me hear three, come on now, that's for the trailer and the load," he started his fast-talking.

Sophie noticed Elijah nod a couple of times, but had no idea that he'd bought the whole mess of stuff until the auctioneer said, "The lot goes to number thirteen standing back there by the pretty red-haired lady for four hundred and fifty dollars."

"Why'd you buy that?" she whispered.

"You might want the fruit jars."

"You idiot! There're dozens and dozens of those in the cellar."

He patted her on the shoulder. "We need another trailer. There're only two on the inventory. With all that land, we'll use at least one more every day. Think about hauling fence posts and barbed wire."

"And what would a new one cost?"

"Up over a thousand."

She nodded. "Then I guess you did good."

"Next item is this riding lawn mower. Good condition. Bought two years ago from Sears. What do I hear? Can we start at two hundred?" His speed-talking started but Elijah didn't raise his hand or his card.

"Sold for three hundred dollars!" he yelled in less than five minutes. "To the lady behind the pretty red-haired woman with the man who bought the trailer. Now moving right along to this plow."

"Buy it," Sophie said.

"Thought I might try," Elijah said.

At the end of the day they owned a trailer, a plow, a small square hay baler, a pickup truck, and all three tractors. Sophie wrote the biggest check on the ranch account that she'd ever written before and handed it to the cashier. But strangely enough, it didn't make her nervous or anxious. The thing that surprised her was that she trusted Elijah so much, when she'd vowed that she'd never trust another man in her entire life.

"We'll deliver it to your ranch tomorrow morning. I expect you'll be driving the truck home, won't you?" the cashier asked.

"Do they always deliver the equipment?" Sophie asked on the way to the truck.

"No, it's a courtesy of this auction. They had it printed on the sale bill that they'd deliver up to two hundred miles on the big equipment. Let's stop in Abilene and get some lunch. What are you hungry for?"

Elijah's voice was full of excitement, like a little boy at Christmas. Just his tone said he could hardly wait to get home and tell the other guys what good deals he'd gotten. He'd gotten all three tractors for the price that he thought he'd have to pay for two, and it didn't take a rocket scientist to see that his feet were about six inches off the ground when he walked beside her.

"Cheap, fast Mexican. Nothing fancy. Just a fast-food place that makes those little dollar tacos. I could eat about eight of them," she said.

"Nervous over spending that much money?"

"No, I am not. When are we going to buy more cows?"

Elijah threw an arm around her shoulders. "One thing at a time, partner."

She flinched.

Not because she wanted him to remove his arm, but she wanted to be more than a partner to Elijah. He darn sure wasn't Prince Charming, but his kisses had awakened her to life and the possibility of love, and "partner" didn't cover nearly enough.

CHAPTER SIXTEEN

Sophie dreamed about Aunt Maud for the first time since the funeral. Her aunt had come to whisper in her ear at the most inopportune times, but she'd never actually dreamed about her in Technicolor until Saturday night. They were sitting at the kitchen table having morning coffee as the sun lit up the sky.

"*It's been more than a month now. You stayin' or sellin'?*" *Aunt Maud asked.*

"*Well, I dang sure ain't goin' nowhere. Elijah won't budge and neither will I.*"

Maud laughed like she did when something was really funny, slapping her leg and wiping at her eyes with her shirttail. "I knew I was doing the right thing. You needed something to shake you out of your doldrums. Eli is just the ticket."

"*I call him Elijah.*"

That brought on more laughter. "Oh, really! Well, darlin', I see good things in your future, and I'm glad you bought that land. This ranch is going to be something else to behold by the time you and Eli pass it on down to the next generation."

And then the dream started to fade and Sophie awoke. No matter how tight she squeezed her eyes shut, she couldn't bring Maud back and there were questions she wanted to ask, answers she needed. She finally popped her eyes open and inhaled deeply. Yep, coffee and bacon and male voices in the kitchen.

She hurriedly dressed in jeans and a bright turquoise tank top, and padded barefoot down the hallway to the big country kitchen. Elijah and his brothers were sitting at the kitchen table, coffee cups in front of them and the pot on a hot pad in the middle of the table. She got her favorite mug from the cabinet, slid into a chair at the other end from Elijah, and poured her own coffee.

"Sleep well?" Hayden asked.

"Dreamed about Aunt Maud," she answered.

"Was she tellin' you the what for?" Tanner asked.

"She was laughing so hard that tears came to her eyes."

Elijah chuckled. "She did pull a pretty slick trick, didn't she?"

Tanner drew his dark brows down in a frown. "Only slick trick I see is that she left half the place to Elijah rather than me. I'm the one who's got the most ranchin' experience, and he's the war vet who was probably going to be a motorcycle bum and ride around the country the rest of his life."

"I'd have ridden around the country for about three months and then reenlisted or done what Jed did and applied at the Bureau." Elijah talked to Tanner but looked down the table into Sophie's eyes.

"I think he means that Aunt Maud pulled a slick trick by leaving half the ranch to Eli and the other half to Sophie. She knew she was tying two cats in a burlap bag and throwing them over a clothesline, and it was her last joke on them," Hayden said.

The light went on in Tanner's eyes. "Oh! Ohhhh!"

"Yep," Hayden nodded.

"What?" Elijah shifted his gaze to his brothers.

"She wanted you two to get together, didn't she?" Tanner said.

"She wanted us to partner up and run this ranch." Elijah blushed.

Sophie giggled.

"What's so funny? Ain't my brother good enough to do more than partner up with you?" Tanner asked.

"She and her friends made this pact thing," Elijah said.

"What?" Tanner looked at Sophie.

"It's a long story," she said.

"We got all mornin'." Hayden refreshed her coffee cup.

"She's got to have a 'life after wife' thing." Elijah's eyes had locked with hers again.

She blinked and looked at Tanner. "It's like this. When Kate, Fancy, and I all moved back to this area, we were talking one night and one of us asked Fancy why she wasn't married. She's tiny and cute and full of life. She said it was because no one had said the three magic words."

Tanner nodded. "'I love you,' right?"

"That's the three words, but not the magic words. We decided that we have to hear that first for sure, but we all three wanted more, a lot more. Fancy wanted someone who'd give her a forever thing, not just a passing fancy that ended up in divorce courts. Kate wanted the three words, but she wanted them from her knight-in-shining...and then she couldn't think of the word 'armor', and said 'whatever,' so we teased her about Hart being her knight-in-shining-whatever."

"And you?" Tanner asked.

"Life after wife."

"What in the devil does that mean?" Hayden asked.

"I was married before. My husband died in a plane crash, but when he got home from his trip I was going to divorce him. He'd been cheating on me since day one of our relationship. I want someone who can give me a life after he gets a wife. Someone who loves me past the wedding day. It's hard to explain."

"I get it," Elijah said.

Hayden scratched his head. "You do?"

"Sure. She wants a marriage, not a wedding. A marriage is two people working together forever. A wedding is the day the marriage is supposed to start, but sometimes, like in Sophie's case, it was the day the relationship died."

Sophie nodded. "So until I'm sure, absolutely sure that I'll have life after wife, then the three words don't mean jack squat to me. So tell me, guys, what're your three magic words?"

Hayden finger-combed his dark hair and set his square jaw seriously. "That's tough. What makes you think we've got three magic words anyway?"

"Everyone has them and, until they figure them out, they don't have any business thinking about settling down," Sophie said.

"I'll have to think about it and get back to you," Tanner said. "Guess I'm not ready to settle down because I thought 'I love you' was the magic. Guess it's just the cupcake. The icing is the magic words."

"That's right," Sophie said. "What about you, Elijah?"

"I'll be faithful," he spit out without hesitation.

"Reason behind it?" she asked.

"He was engaged when he went to the desert the second time. He wasn't gone a week when his woman was flirtin' around in a bar with another man. A month later she sent him a breakup note," Hayden said.

"She broke up with him on Facebook!" Tanner said. "Put it right out there for everyone to see and mailed the ring to Momma rather than coming around and facing my folks."

Sophie's interest was piqued, but Elijah looked like he was about to crawl under the table or else set the whole kitchen on fire with his red face.

"You deserve better, Elijah," she said and abruptly changed the subject. "What's on everyone's agenda today? Tomorrow we really get down to business now that the new equipment is here, but what are y'all doin' today?"

Hayden refilled his cup. "I'm watchin' a football game while my laundry runs, and maybe getting my sleeping quarters put into shape. I think my laptop got put out in storage, so I may spend some time out there searching for it. I'm addicted to e-mail."

Tanner shrugged. "Same thing, I guess. I might take that new tractor out around the fence line just to get the feel of how it drives."

"Elijah and I are going over to Theron and Fancy's place this afternoon. He wants to look at some cattle, and the girls and I have our gossip fest on Sunday if everyone can make it," Sophie said.

Hayden stood up and stretched the kinks from his back and neck. He was almost as tall as Elijah and maybe ten pounds heavier. Still handsome enough to make women take a second or third look with his dark looks and thick lashes over dark brown eyes. Tanner did the same. He was plainly Hayden's twin, but his face was slightly thinner, his eyes a lighter brown, and his hair had a bit of wave in it.

It hadn't taken Sophie long to figure out their differences, and now she had no trouble telling them apart. Besides Tanner's lighter eyes, he was the one who spoke up the fastest while Hayden was the deeper thinker.

"Hungry?" Elijah asked Sophie when they were gone.

"Are there leftovers?"

"No, but there's still pancake batter in the bowl and the griddle is on the stove," he answered.

She pushed back her chair and headed to the kitchen. "Pancakes sound good. How do you take them?"

"I've already eaten. Me and the boys had breakfast together."

She smiled.

His heart did one of those crazy flip-flops that constricted his chest muscles.

She went on, "I figured that much. I like mine with butter, applesauce, and then a little syrup drizzled over the top. I was asking you how you like yours."

"Melted butter and lots of maple syrup," he answered.

She filed that away for the next Sunday when she planned to do the cooking. Maybe she'd treat them to her pumpkin pancakes or the new recipe she and Maud discovered using ground pecans. Both went exceptionally well with maple syrup.

She was still thinking about cooking when the fine hair on her neck prickled and she turned quickly to find herself in Elijah's arms. He'd taken the coffeepot to the cabinet and was peering over her shoulder, watching her flip pancakes and then his arms were around her. She turned slowly without making him loosen his hold. Their gazes locked. Her gray eyes searched deeply into his blue ones, and then their lips connected in a passionate kiss that left her knees weak and her heart about to jump plumb out of her chest and do a jig on the floor.

"I was about to make another pot of coffee. I expect you'll need some after all that sweet syrup," he whispered hoarsely.

She cocked her head to one side and shimmied out of his arms. How in the great green earth could he kiss her like that and then talk about coffee? If her kisses affected him the way his did her, he wouldn't be able to utter a sane word, much less talk about coffee! She could have strangled the man until he turned blue and then slapped him for changing colors.

Life was not fair! She should have listened to common sense the first time she saw him on that motorcycle at Maud's funeral. It said to shoot the man. Now she'd let him inch his way into her heart and had no idea how to get him out.

Elijah had just about lost his socks when he kissed Sophie. It happened every time their lips touched. He hadn't come to Baird looking for anything but a quiet, busy life of ranching. He certainly hadn't planned on falling for the sassy redhead determined to send him packing off to another ranch. But he had and now he didn't have any idea what to do about it.

If he started a relationship with her, she'd always wonder if it was because he really wanted her half of the ranch. He didn't have a doubt that he could trust her and that she would be faithful. After the way she'd been treated in the past, she would never enter into a relationship without being totally sure that it was the right thing and that it was eternal.

Eternal, Elijah thought as he busied himself at the kitchen sink, rinsing the coffeepot. Mercy, was he really thinking of something long-term with Sophie McSwain? Could he even think the *M word* without getting hives?

After he'd gotten the message from his ex-fiancé, he'd vowed he'd never trust another woman. And yet, there he was, thinking Sophie and marriage in the same sentence and there wasn't a single itchy splotch on him. When and where had he fallen for the woman?

It sure hadn't been love at first sight. He'd been sure she would take his money and take off for the nearest shopping mall, but he'd been wrong. He frowned as he tried to remember the first time they'd even been civil to each other.

It had only been five weeks, but he felt as if he'd known her his whole life, and it had happened slowly over the hours and days of working side by side. Now what in the devil was he supposed to do with it?

Could he offer her the life after wife that she wanted? She deserved it and more. She was the hardest working woman he knew, maybe even more so than his mother had been. Sophie would crawl up on a tractor, get her hands dirty changing oil or transmission fluid, and bale hay with the best of the hired hands. And then she could dress up in her Western boots and fancy clothes and fit into his arms like they were made for dancing together.

"Whatever are you thinking about?" she asked, breaking into his inner thoughts.

He jumped. "Fishin'."

"Well, you've washed that pot three times. I reckon it's clean." She piled the last pancake on a plate and carried it to the table.

He chuckled. "Guess I was doin' some powerful woolgathering."

"Evidently. I've made too many pancakes. Get a fork and come help me eat them."

"Couldn't possibly put another bite in my overloaded stomach. I'm going out to the tack room to gather up all our fishin' gear. We'll take the new truck."

"We usually meet about one at Fancy's place. I'd planned on doing laundry and some housework until twelve thirty or so. That fit with your plans?"

"Just fine." He put on a pot of coffee and disappeared out the back door. Maybe there would be answers out in the tack room for all the questions that kiss had raised up in his soul.

CHAPTER SEVENTEEN

Kate and Hart were already at Fancy and Theron's ranch when Elijah and Sophie arrived. Hart and Theron were leaning on a corral fence and motioned Elijah over that way when he and Sophie were out of the truck.

She hurried into the house and was greeted by Kate rocking Glory Emma-Gwen in the corner of the kitchen, Fancy pulling fresh chocolate chip cookies from the oven, and Tina dancing around like she had ants in her pants asking when the cookies would be cool enough to eat.

Normality, and she loved it. After Elijah's kiss that morning she was almost too antsy to even eat pancakes, and now she was starving again because she hadn't bothered with lunch. She took three glasses from the cabinet, filled them with ice from the freezer, and poured some sweet tea.

"I expect you're going to fuss about it being your turn to hold the baby," Kate said.

"You expect right," Sophie said.

Tina hopped on one foot. "Well, I want the cookies to hurry up so I can take some to Daddy. Momma said I could take them all by myself when they got unhot."

"It's not fair," Kate said. "You got two daughters, and I don't even have one."

Fancy pushed back a strand of blonde hair and smiled. "You know what to do about that, girlfriend."

"I'm waiting on Sophie," Kate said.

Sophie almost dropped the two glasses of tea she was carrying to the table. "Well, darlin', you might die childless if you are waiting on me."

"Hmmph," Kate snorted.

Tina bounced around from Kate, where she peeked at her new baby sister; to Sophie, where she begged to carry the last glass to the kitchen table; to Fancy, where she wanted to put ice on the cookies to cool them.

"OK, antsy britches, I reckon I can put a few on a paper plate and you can take them out to the horse corral. Your daddy said he'd even saddle up your pony and let you ride around the corral this afternoon," Fancy said.

Tina jumped up and down like a windup toy in excitement. "Someday when I get bigger, Daddy says I can go out of the corral on my pony, and then I'm going to ride all the way to see y'all."

"That's a long way," Sophie said.

Tina settled down and looked up at Sophie, her big brown eyes serious. "My pony can ride a long time without getting tired."

"Then I'll be glad to see you comin' down the lane," Sophie said and winked at Fancy.

Tina carried the cookies out the door very carefully. Kate stood up and handed the baby to Sophie, who immediately claimed the rocking chair.

The way that the baby fit into her arms sent her biological clock ticking so loud that it almost deafened her. She'd always wanted a big family, maybe even five or six children instead of the usual two or three, but her husband had wanted to make sure his career was solid before they started down that path. At least that was the story she got. But she wasn't going to think about that; she was going to smell fresh baby powder and relish the moments she could hold a sweet little girl.

"And now it is confessional time," Kate said. "We want to hear every single detail of the date. And remember we are all BFFs, and if you leave out a single little thing, we'll know, and we will fix you up this coming Friday night."

"It didn't really start out as a date. We've decided to pool our money and buy the two ranches just south of the Double Bar M. They got burned pretty bad, and the owners are wanting to sell. So Elijah asked me if I'd like to ride down to the Dairy Queen for ice cream to celebrate our decision," she said.

Fancy sat down at the table and wolfed down two cookies. "Don't sound like a date to me. There's a new youth minister at our church. He's got pretty green eyes and he's about our age. I'm calling him tomorrow."

"No, it was a date. I promise," Sophie said quickly.

Kate downed her third cookie. "Tell us more and we'll decide."

"We had ice cream and wound up sharing the last scoop of my banana split," Sophie said.

"Still not sure if it's a full-fledged date," Fancy said.

"Let me finish. I loved the motorcycle. Even thought about buying one after I'd ridden on his, with my arms around his waist, I might add. Is it getting closer to a date?"

Fancy twisted her full mouth off to one side.

Kate drew her black eyebrows down.

"So since I loved the ride so much, we went up to Fort Griffin," and she went on to tell them every single detail she could think of—up to and including the kiss.

"Any more kisses since then?" Kate asked.

Sophie held up two fingers.

"Then I guess you're off the hook until next week. But if there aren't at least three kisses a week between now and then, Fancy is talking to the youth director," Kate said.

"You are both…" Sophie couldn't think of anything vile enough.

"Pigs from…" Kate started one of their favorite lines from *Steel Magnolias*.

"Hades," Fancy hurried and finished the line without using bad language.

"Yes, you are," Sophie said. "And for being so demanding and such good friends at the same time, next Saturday is when we're all going to Abilene to a trailer place to find my new home. I'm tired of living in a house where I wake up every morning to men's voices in my kitchen."

Kate handed her a cookie. "He's not your life after wife?"

"Too soon to tell, and I need my own space."

"If I wasn't married, I wouldn't mind waking up to three sexy cowboys in my kitchen every day. Those brothers of his would make a holy woman's panty hose start falling down," Kate giggled.

"Yeah, if Elijah ain't the one, then maybe Hayden or Tanner is." Fancy laughed with Kate.

Sophie looked at both of them like they'd developed a third eye right in the middle of their foreheads. "You are both certifiably goofy."

That set them off into more giggles.

Fancy wiped her eyes with a dish towel and said, "Sounds like true love to me. How about you, Kate?"

"Speaking from my experience, I'd say it's about time to put the two of you out on a Louisiana swamp island like Granny did me and Hart," Kate said.

"No, thank you," Sophie declared.

"You'd be amazed at how much thinkin' you can do when you are fishin'," Kate said.

"Really? That's where we are going today when we leave here. He's got a boat lined up over at the lake, and the fishin' gear is in back of the truck. I've got a book in my tote bag in case I get bored," Sophie told her.

"Bored! Honey, if you get bored, you come on home and stake out a claim on one of them other Jones boys or else the youth minister. I figured out a lot with a fishin' pole in my hands when me and Hart were trying to get over the speed bumps of life," Kate said.

Sophie looked at Fancy. "You and Theron been fishin'?"

She shook her head. "No, we got stuck in a cabin back in the boondocks during an ice storm, remember?"

It was Sophie's turn to nod. She wasn't sure that fishing or spending time in an iced-in cabin would convince her that Elijah Jones was the man for her, or that he was able to offer her a life after wife. There were moments when she was slyly watching him that dark shadows passed over his face and his eyes went dull. Times like those, she wondered if he was reliving bad experiences from the war. Maybe it wasn't that he wouldn't offer her what she needed to say those two words again, but that he was afraid to let anyone into his heart. In that case, she sure wished he'd keep his kisses to himself.

"Did you hear me?" Fancy touched her on the leg.

"I'm sorry, I was woolgathering. What did you say?"

"I said that your aunt Maud knew exactly what she was doing when she left the ranch to both of you. She was a wise old girl," Fancy said.

A knock on the back door caused them all to look that way. Elijah was standing on the other side of the old-fashioned screen door with a big grin on his face. "You about ready to go, Sophie? The wind has died down, and it's a perfect day for catfish to bite."

"I'll see you girls next Saturday." Sophie handed the baby off to Kate who already had her arms out. "Meet me at the ranch at ten o'clock. Fancy, bring the kids. We'll put their car seats over in my truck. Plenty of room."

"Oh, no!" Fancy said. "I'm keeping the nanny all day and having a day out with just y'all. That's what Tina has taken to calling the housekeeper."

❧ ❧ ❧

Elijah couldn't have wiped the smile off his face if it had meant doing it or eating dirt. Sophie looked so darned cute sitting in that rocking chair with that baby in her arms. He could visualize her with a child of her own, maybe with his blue eyes and her red hair, rocking him to sleep at night.

Him! His mother's voice crawled inside his head. *What makes you think you're going to have sons like your father did? You might wind up with a house full of girl children, and they'll sure enough make you pay for your raising, son.*

The smile disappeared in an instant. Girls! He'd never thought of girl babies. Actually, he'd never thought of children until that very moment. But he liked the idea, and there was still time for him to experience fatherhood…if he didn't drag his feet too long.

CHAPTER EIGHTEEN

They were on their way to the lake when Elijah's phone started playing "Good Directions." He dug it out of his shirt pocket, flipped it open, and answered. He listened for a few seconds, tossed the phone on the dash, whipped a U-turn right in the middle of the road, and stomped the gas pedal.

"Place to the north of us has a grass fire. Tanner is plowing a firebreak right up next to the road as a precaution, and Hayden is herding cattle to the south. It's not huge yet, since the wind isn't blowing like last time, but we'd better get on back," he explained.

Sophie held onto the armrest, disappointment filling her heart and soul. After what Kate said, she'd looked forward to a fishing trip. Now it looked as if her Sunday afternoon would be spent fighting fire again.

"It's leased land. The owners retired to Arizona last year and leased it to the folks who live across the road. The house has been up for rent. Last renters moved out at the end of the school year. Couple of teachers who decided Baird wasn't for them. I suppose you'll be wanting to buy it next?" she asked.

"I'll buy all that we can afford," he answered.

He slowed down in Albany, but it wasn't easy to go the speed limit. When they were back out on the highway, he eased the gas pedal down until they were going eighty. Sophie sighed when she saw gray smoke spiraling toward the sky out ahead.

"I'm only ten miles over the speed limit," he snapped.

"I wasn't sighing because of buying the land or the speed you are driving," she snapped right back at him.

This wasn't the way the day was meant to go. They were supposed to have a lazy afternoon together. Sophie was going to think about things between her and Elijah, not fight with him. She was going to lie back in the sun with her straw hat shading her eyes and catch a catfish for supper, then tease Elijah because her fish was bigger than his.

"Then why were you sighing?" he asked.

"Smoke. Fire. I hate fighting fire, and it's a constant worry in this part of the country when things are so dry. I'd love a wet spring, wet summer, and no drought, but this is Texas and I might as well wish for…" She stopped midsentence.

Elijah slowed down enough to slide around the corner into the lane leading back to the ranch. Smoke was as thick as fog and about the same color. There were no two-story flames dancing across the dry pasture. They came to a screeching halt in front of the house, and she didn't hear the pained bawling of cows to the north, only the aggravated carrying-on of those being herded to safety back behind the house.

She hopped out of the truck, grabbed her straw hat, and crammed it on her head. "I'll take the old tractor and start on up by the highway. Looks like Hayden has got the new one cuttin' a groove toward the east."

"I'll go help Tanner herd cattle." Elijah headed to the barn where the four-wheelers and horses were kept. Four-wheelers were better in the case of fire because it spooked the horses, so he mounted one and took off toward the south of the ranch.

It was near supper time when they all four met at the house. Kendall, Randy, and Frankie drove up just as they were walking up on the porch, and Tanner shot them a dirty look.

"Hey, don't look at me like that," Frankie said. "If you would've called, we'd have been here sooner. We didn't even know there was a fire until we was coming home."

Home! The word struck Sophie so hard that it brought tears to her eyes. The guys thought of the ranch as home already and that was where family resided.

"You kids stop your bickering. I don't know how your momma raised nine of you." She looked at Elijah. "Hayden, you and Tanner get on out to the bunkhouse and wash the smoke out of your hair and change clothes. You other three get on in the house before you get the smell on you. Elijah, me and you are going to have a shower, and then we're going to make supper. We can all eat in the house tonight."

Elijah wiggled his dusty eyebrows.

Sophie cocked her head to one side and then it hit her.

"Not together! Good grief! I don't have time for your shenanigans any more than I do the kids. You go on and get a shower first. I'll put a couple of frozen lasagnas in the oven and get a salad cut up. Mercy! Living with boys! I'm glad I never had brothers." She mumbled as she headed toward the kitchen.

Elijah whistled all the way to the bathroom. He took a quick shower, shaved for the second time that day, and applied Stetson aftershave. He dressed in fresh jeans and a knit, three-button blue shirt the same color as his eyes, and brushed his black hair back. He'd be glad when it grew back out a little, especially since Sophie had made that comment about liking it longer.

When he reached the kitchen, she had already slid two big pans of lasagna in the oven, washed a head of lettuce, and was chopping tomatoes and green onions. He took the knife from her hands and was only slightly amazed at the tingle when their fingers brushed in the transfer.

"Go on and get your shower now. I'll take over here. Garlic bread?"

She nodded. "And when the timer goes off, put that cobbler in the oven. We'll have it warm with ice cream for dessert."

She hurried down the hallway, but even rushing didn't take the scent of his aftershave from her nostrils, and it sure didn't do a thing for her already speeding pulse.

Elijah moved right into the position of cook with ease, and while the salad chilled, he whipped garlic with butter, slathered it on thick slices of Italian bread, and wrapped it all in foil. When the timer buzzed, he removed the lasagna pans and slid the cobbler into the oven, reset the timer, and set the dining room table for seven.

That's what the table would look like if me and Sophie had five kids, he thought.

"Holy smoke, what am I doing?" he muttered. "It's this living in close quarters and not seeing other women for days on end. I couldn't live with that woman. She's got a temper."

And you don't? His mother was back in his head arguing with him again. *I like Sophie. You'll never have a dull moment if you spend the rest of your life with her. She'll keep you on your toes, son.*

"Yeah, right!" he said aloud.

"Right what?" Sophie asked from the hallway.

His mouth felt like he'd just eaten alum pie. If he was forced to speak or be shot, he would have had to put on the blindfold and get ready to feel the bullets. She was wearing a white sundress with straps that tied on her shoulders. Her red hair was still damp, and kinky curls floated on her shoulders. And she smelled like something between heaven and angels.

"Who were you talking to?" Sophie asked.

"Momma," he said before he thought. Mercy, the woman would think he was daft talking to his dead mother.

"She messin' with your thoughts? Aunt Maud does that to me. She pops into my head like that crazy old aunt on those *Bewitched* reruns on late-night television. Remember how she used to pop in and out of Samantha's house because she never could get her spells right?"

Elijah inhaled deeply and got another whiff of her perfume mixed with something tropical, like coconut and pineapple, that she must've used on her hair. He nodded and headed back to the kitchen with her right behind him.

"Aunt Maud ever fuss at you?" she asked.

"Nope," he said.

"What was your momma tellin' you?" she asked.

He finally found his voice. "To put the knives on the right side of the plates."

It was a lie, but he couldn't very well tell her what his mother was really talking to him about, now could he?

The back door opened and Hayden and Tanner came pushing into the kitchen. More Stetson. More soap smells. Just proof positive that Sophie needed her own place and soon!

❖ ❖ ❖

Life after Wife

Elijah paced the floor.

The week had flown by so fast that he wondered if it had sprouted wings. The new fence was coming along, and the pasture on the new property was losing a lot of mesquite trees. Hayden had found a rental place in Abilene and had a bulldozer delivered on Monday, and every day all week he'd reclaimed ground. The progress was phenomenal, and he was talking about renting the machine for another week.

Hayden and Tanner had left right at noon for Silverton to pick up a few more of their things and to see their older brothers. Randy, Frankie, and Kendall were off to visit their families. For the first time in months Elijah was alone.

And he paced the floor.

Back and forth from the living room to the kitchen, through the dining room and back to the living room, down the hall to his bedroom, then into his office where he toyed with a game on the computer for all of thirty seconds before he was up pacing again.

Sophie had gone with the girls to trailer shop. He'd known about it all week, and what it meant hadn't hit him exactly until she waved at him from the truck. He'd been sitting in Aunt Maud's rocking chair on the porch and, the minute she waved, it was as if she was telling him good-bye for good.

She'd bring home the deed and title to a double-wide, and in a few short weeks, she'd be out of the house. Already it was as quiet as a tomb and just as cold, even though the thermometer on the porch post said it was eighty-five degrees. It was another hot one for the last week in September.

Two months before he would have given Sophie his entire paycheck to get off the Double Bar M; now he wondered how he'd survive in the house without her. What had annoyed

207

him to the point of homicide a few weeks ago was suddenly endearing and cute.

He checked the time on a pass-through of the kitchen. Barely one o'clock. They'd just be reaching Abilene about now, and she'd be looking over the first of the double-wide homes. Sophie didn't belong in a trailer. What if a tornado hit the area? Everyone knew those things weren't safe in a tornado.

He picked up his phone from the cabinet and sent her a text: *Have you thought about tornadoes?*

One came back immediately: *They said they tie these down so they're safe. Guaranteed!*

He wanted to stomp the phone, but instead he tucked it into his pocket and headed for the tack room in the barn. Time would pass far quicker if he didn't have a clock to keep checking and if he kept his hands busy. There was always tack to be polished, and, last time he checked the room, it looked like a real tornado had wound its way through there.

Determined to make it spotless and get everything organized, he dove into the work with the gusto of a hunting hound on the trail of a coyote. But as is often the case when the hands are busy, the mind takes off on a trip of its own. At two o'clock Elijah sent another text message: *Found one yet?*

One came back: *You in a hurry to get me out of the house?*

He sat down and propped his feet up on the worktable and typed with his thumbs: *No, I am not.*

She sent one back: *Gathering brochures. You can help me choose when I get home. We're off to the mall, but Fancy has to be back at five.*

"Three hours," he moaned.

He led Wild Bill, the big black horse that Maud bought just before she died, out of his stall and saddled him up. Maybe a ride around all three sections of land would take three hours and clear his mind.

Fightin' with your heart is always a tough battle, his mother said as he cinched up the saddle.

"Yes, but maybe my heart shouldn't win," he said.

❖ ❖ ❖

Sophie arrived at the ranch to find everything eerily quiet. The stillness was even more pronounced by the fact that she'd just left her friends where they were talking and giggling all at once about her new home options.

Kate thought she should build a mansion on the southernmost part of the new property. Fancy's idea was that she should abandon it all and kick Elijah out to the bunkhouse. Sophie dropped her purse and the brochures on the kitchen table, made a hurried trip to the bathroom, and noticed that both Elijah's bedroom door and his office door were open.

She'd looked forward to getting his input on the new double-wide, and she'd brought home a whole stack of brochures. She'd told him that, so where was he?

She meandered out to the back porch, shaded her eyes with the back of her hand, and noticed the barn door was open so she headed that way, expecting him to see her walking across the pasture and come meet her.

But she reached the barn without seeing anything of Elijah. His pickup was in the front yard, but maybe he'd gone off somewhere with Hart. She was so disappointed that she could have cried.

The two horses that lived at the ranch had been stabled in the barn since the fire. She checked the stalls and Wild Bill was gone. That was a mean thing for Elijah to do, go for a ride at the very time he knew she'd be home. Evidently, he didn't want to be included in her plans and that disappointed her all over again.

She was on her way back to the house when she heard hoof beats coming from the south. She shaded her eyes again and could see a black blur with a cowboy coming at her in a dead run. Wild Bill enjoyed a good run, and so did Elijah from the way he'd let the horse have rein to go as fast as he wanted.

She kept walking. No need for her to stay in the barn while Elijah spent at least thirty minutes removing the saddle and rubbing the sweaty horse down. At least he treated Aunt Maud's horse right when he let him run like the wind. Too bad he didn't treat his friends the same way.

The hoof beats got closer and closer and suddenly horse and rider bypassed her. The horse jumped the yard fence and came to a halt at the back door, where Elijah slid out of the saddle and waved at her.

She took her own sweet time getting to the yard gate, opened it slowly, and locked gazes with Elijah. His eyes were dancing, so evidently he'd enjoyed his fast ride. The horse's flanks heaved as he cooled down, but his eyes said that he'd do it again if the cowboy would just mount up and let him jump over that fence.

"Good ride?" she asked.

"Oh, yeah! Cleared my mind right up. I'll take him out to the barn and rub him down, but I think it's all right now to turn him and the mare out in the pasture around the barn. What do you think?" Elijah asked breathlessly.

"If you think it's time, then have at it," she said.

"I'll be back in half an hour. Would you please meet me on the porch with some sweet tea and your brochures? I'm really interested in your day, but I wasn't expectin' you home until five."

She remembered that she had told him five, but that was when Fancy had to be back at her ranch. She should have been more definite as to when she'd be home. Her spirits lifted and she nodded.

She made a fresh pitcher of tea, filled two glasses with ice, put it all on a tray, and carried it to the front porch. The wind had died down to a gentle breeze picking up the fall aroma of yellow, gold, and burgundy mums blooming around the front porch and a few yellow roses still lingering at the end of the house.

The brochures showed a dozen double-wide trailers, and the man said that he could get one set up and ready to live in within a month. Plumbing, electricity, and a foundation of concrete blocks had to be taken care of before the actual moving date. That would give her time to buy furniture, curtains, and her own towels.

The first one showed her favorite. Three bedrooms, a Jacuzzi in the master bathroom, and a walk-in closet. But suddenly the future did not loom happy. Instead it looked lonely and bleak. No rough old cowboys piled up in her living room watching television in the evenings. No making Sunday supper for the "kids."

"Hey." Elijah came from around the end of the house.

He smelled like horse, barn, tack room, the remnants of shaving lotion, and sweat, and she loved every bit of it. His straight black hair stuck up all over his head and there was a dirt smudge below his left eye.

"Thirsty?" she asked.

"Yes, ma'am."

She poured two glasses of tea and handed him one. He downed the whole thing before coming up for air.

"Very good."

She took the glass from his hand and handed him a brochure. He propped a hip on the porch railing and studied it all of ten seconds before handing it back to her.

"Is this what you really want? To live alone so me and the guys won't be a bother? Please be honest."

She shook her head...honestly.

Elijah dropped down on one knee beside her. "I've been out riding for more than two hours getting my thoughts together. I didn't plan on falling in love with you when Aunt Maud left me half of this place, but I did. I'm forty years old, and I want a family. I want it with you, Sophie McSwain."

She was stunned speechless.

"And?" she finally whispered.

"Will you marry me? I don't have a ring. I just figured most of this out while you were gone, and I realized that I do not want you to move out. I want you in my life, in my house forever, because you are already in my heart. I'm not romantic, but I can promise you life after wife. I will always be faithful, and I'll never leave you. That does not mean we won't fight and argue, but it does mean that I'll cherish you above every other thing or person in this world."

"When did you know?" she asked.

"The first time I kissed you, but it took me a while to figure it all out," he said.

She leaned forward and wrapped her arms around Elijah's neck, pulling his lips to hers in a kiss. "Yes, darlin', I will marry you, and I've been fightin' it as long as you have."

Sophie could have sworn she heard Aunt Maud sigh and then a gentle breeze carried it away.

They were married Monday morning at the Shackelford County Courthouse in Albany with a janitor and the county clerk serving as witnesses. On the way home Sophie called Fancy and told her that she didn't need to fix her up with the youth director because she and Elijah had just gotten married.

Fancy squealed and then said, "Please let me call Kate. She's never going to believe this. And, darlin', there will be a reception in a few weeks right here on my ranch."

When they arrived at the Double Bar M, Elijah picked her up like a bride and carried her over the threshold. He didn't stop in the living room but kept going until they reached his bedroom.

"Welcome home, Mrs. Jones," he whispered, and then kissed her hard before setting her on the floor inside his bedroom.

She pulled his face to hers for another kiss. "Yes, we *are* home, aren't we?"

"And today begins the first day of your life after wife, darlin'." He kicked the bedroom door shut with his boot heel.

The End

ACKNOWLEDGMENTS

Dear Readers,

It's never easy to end a trilogy or a series. Saying good-bye to characters is like leaving a family reunion and knowing you won't see all the cousins, aunts, uncles, and friends for a long time. But the Three Magic Words trilogy comes to an end with Sophie and Elijah's story. I hope that you've enjoyed visiting that part of Texas and getting to know Fancy, Kate, and Sophie, and all the folks that played a part in their stories.

During the writing of this trilogy, I made several trips to that part of Texas. I ate at the café in Albany, slept at the Ridge Motel, and walked on the courthouse lawn in Breckinridge. My husband and I drove through Baird and waved back at several ranchers who lifted their hands to us in greeting as our trucks passed along the back roads. Folks were friendly and helpful and proved again that small towns have a heartbeat and pulse of their own.

Thanks goes to everyone that has had a hand in making this book possible, especially the warm and supportive staff at Montlake Romance. Also to my husband, who is always ready at the drop of a hat to go with me on research trips so I get the details just right.

Most of all, thank you to all my readers. Thank you for reading my books, for buying them, for sharing them with your neighbors, for talking about them in your book clubs. and for the notes that you send to me after you've read them. Until next time,

Carolyn Brown

ABOUT THE AUTHOR

Carolyn Brown lives in southern Oklahoma with her husband, three grown children, and enough grandchildren to keep her young. When she's not scrambling to meet writing deadlines, she enjoys walking through her husband's flower gardens. Her novel *Love Drunk Cowboy* is a *New York Times* and *USA Today* bestseller, *Getting Lucky* was a Romance Studio CAPA nominee, and *The Ladies' Room* was a RITA finalist.

Photo by Charles Brown, 2012

Made in the USA
Charleston, SC
15 January 2013